GENE INYART NAMOVICZ

TO TALK IN TIME

FOUR WINDS PRESS　　NEW YORK

12574

With special thanks to

EVELYN WAINWRIGHT TURPIN
who lent me an island

and to

LARRY CALLEN
who found me a villain

ACKNOWLEDGMENTS

I would like to thank Patricia Randall at the Information Office of the National Institute of Allergy and Infectious Diseases, and Rex Naylor, former Chief of Speech Pathology at the Bethesda Naval Hospital. What I have done right in their areas of expertise is due to them. (What I may have done wrong is my own fault.)

I would also like to thank Lucy Parker for saving the lives of hundreds of sick and ailing wild birds, and for answering my questions about the doctoring and feeding of same.

Four Winds Press, Macmillan Publishing Company, 866 Third Avenue, New York, NY 10022. Collier Macmillan Canada, Inc.

First Edition. Printed in the United States of America   10 9 8 7 6 5 4 3 2 1

The text of this book is set in 12 pt. Bembo. Library of Congress Cataloging-in-Publication Data • Namovicz, Gene Inyart. To talk in time. Summary: Paralyzed into silence whenever he has to speak to anyone he doesn't know very well, twelve-year-old Luke is forced to face his fears in order to protect a passing stranger from rabies. [1. Emotional problems—Fiction. 2. Speech—Disorders—Fiction. 3. Rabies—Fiction. 4. Islands—Fiction] I. Title.
PZ7.N1427T3   1987   [Fic]   86–18481   ISBN 0–02–768170–X

CHAPTER ONE

WHAT woke Luke was the car not moving anymore. Through half-open eyes he saw the mashed McDonald's bag on the floor mat and knew at once where he was— where they were going.

"How close are we now?" he mumbled sleepily.

When Paul didn't answer, Luke unglued his sweaty face from the top suitcase and sat up. The front seat was empty and the car was parked at one of those places with six rows of gas pumps, a giant snack bar, and a five-acre parking lot. Outside the car window bees dive-bombed a big green trash bin. Next to the bin was a sign pointing to the rest rooms, so it wasn't hard to figure out where his brother had gone. After the sixteen-ounce Pepsi Luke had drunk when they stopped for lunch, he was ready to go, too. Groggily, he opened the door and stepped out onto the hot tarmac.

"Hello, there! You people been driving all day?"

Luke stiffened and he felt the familiar dryness in his mouth. All of a sudden his hands got sweaty. The voice sounded like a fairly old woman. Grandmothers always tried to start a conversation and were the hardest to shake off. His chin raised ever so slightly, Luke turned to look at her.

"Good to get out and stretch your legs, isn't it?" she said.

Luke managed a nod. The woman sure wasn't stretching anything. She sat like a lump on a flimsy-looking folding chair in the shade of a shining white Winnebago. When their eyes met, she let her newspaper fall closed and gave him an expectant smile.

Luke's gaze slid away from hers to the books scattered around the front seat of the Volvo. He needed a way to look busy. In a businesslike manner, he opened the car door and began to collect them—Paul's own textbooks and the medical books he had gotten from their grandfather. What was taking Paul so long? The inside of the car was already an oven; if he had to close it, they'd broil when they got back in. But he couldn't walk away and leave it unlocked. Or could he? That woman was all eyes and ears. No one would dare carry off their suitcases and stuff while she was sitting there. Anyway, he really had to go.

Leaving the windows open, Luke slammed the car door and jogged off in the direction the sign pointed, sort of smiling at the woman as he passed her. He expected to run into Paul on the way, but he didn't, and he didn't see him in the men's room either.

Back out in the fresh air a few minutes later, he stepped off the sidewalk, out of the way of people coming and going. As he stood there, staring at the weedy blue flowers along the curb, he was startled to see a small boy—grinning from ear to ear—careening toward him on a skateboard.

"Catch him!" a man's voice called.

Luke spread his feet apart and leaned forward to block the boy. He knew he had to do it—otherwise the skateboard would shoot out among the moving cars—but he really hated to spoil the kid's ride.

"*No!*" A hard little head slammed into Luke's midriff and two fists hammered his hands aside. "No! No! No!" the little boy screamed in protest, but by then the father was there, ready to take him, kicking and crying, from Luke's arms.

"Thanks! Thanks a lot! He's a trip, Joey is. You have to watch him—watch him every minute. We were just sitting down to have a picnic when he took off."

A boy of thirteen or fourteen ran up to rescue the skateboard, overturned in the dry grass with its wheels still spinning. "Took off from the top of the embankment yet," he muttered, smiling at Luke sourly. "Thanks."

Luke ducked his head in apology to little Joey—who didn't notice because his eyes were squinched closed in a howl of rage—and headed back to the Volvo.

He felt good. He'd waited a long time for today, deliberately holding back his excitement because it wasn't safe to hope. "We're keeping the cottage, Luke," his mother had said when they moved away last year. "We'll come back every summer." She'd meant it, too. Then. She loved the island as much as he did. But when Dad got an offer to help excavate another old shipwreck just off Cyprus, Luke knew he'd been right not to count on the promise. His father's eyes had glowed when he told them. "They think it's fourth century. You understand why I can't pass up the chance, don't you?"

Luke understood. He understood, but he felt like a balloon with a slow leak until Paul rescued him as he had so many times before—like when Luke fell off the seawall at high tide when he was only three. Paul saved him again by telling Mom and Dad that he would go back to the island and work his old job one more summer. And take Luke with him.

Luke laughed out loud as a sea gull glided across the parking lot. No, not a gull. . . . It was too good a glider—too streamlined. It had to be a tern. Either way, it was a sign that they were getting nearer. Somewhere up the road was the ocean.

He walked faster. As he turned the corner, the big white Winnebago moved slowly past the last bank of gas pumps and headed toward the highway exit. Luke frowned. There went his watchman—watchwoman—but Paul must have come back by now. Paul was probably all set to go, waiting for him.

Luke stopped cold. Where was the Volvo? The Winnebago was gone. He'd seen it leave. But the cream-colored station wagon was still parked at the corner across from the buses. The red truck was in its same spot. And there was the sign pointing to the rest rooms.

He crouched on the curb, making himself think things through. Don't panic, he told himself. After all, he'd only been gone three or four minutes at most—in and out of the men's room in nothing flat, then a quick stop to field the little kid on the way back. Paul hadn't had time to get impatient and go looking for him. Maybe he'd driven over to the snack bar to buy them some hamburgers, or maybe he'd gone for gas. Whichever, wherever, he was sure to come right back. Luke took a deep breath, all calmed down. Then he glanced over at the gas station and panicked.

The Volvo wasn't at the pumps and it wasn't headed back to pick him up. Instead, it was rolling merrily toward the access road. Paul was leaving without him.

Luke started running. He cut across the parking lot and nearly got clipped by a tractor trailer pulling away from the pumps. The driver yelled at him but Luke didn't break stride. He kept pounding along, pumping with his arms, past a slow-moving Honda, knowing all the time that he wasn't going to make it. He could see Paul easing the car onto I-95. . . .

He stopped running at the end of the exit drive. While he stood there gasping for breath, the Volvo roared out of sight.

CHAPTER TWO

FOR a few seconds Luke's eyes blurred. His chest heaved and he had to fight to get his breath. A Greyhound bus, loaded with people, came along and the driver honked at him. Luke moved numbly to the side of the road to let the bus pass.

Then the rage hit him. Stupid bus driver! What was the blazing rush? Luke clenched his fist and pounded it into his other hand as hard as he could—over and over again. *Dumb! Dumb! Dumb! He* was the idiot! Why hadn't he closed the Volvo and locked it? Then Paul would have seen that he was gone—would have waited for him.

"Anything wrong, buddy?"

Luke stared up at a friendly-looking truck driver, bewildered. He knew that the guy leaning out of the cab window just wanted to help, but he didn't need help. Paul would come back for him. Until he did, Luke could take care of himself. Forcing a grin, he waved the trucker on and strode away from the gas pumps. Better wait near the snack bar. People were crowded around there all the time and he wouldn't stand out as much. Then he hesitated. Maybe he ought to start walking after

Paul. It would be better than waiting here. Or would it? He'd have to cross the median to the southbound road—the one that Paul would use coming back. He'd be face-to-face with the traffic—but he still might miss the Volvo.

Out of the corner of his eye, he saw a car drawing near, slowing down. Someone else wondering about him, probably. Who's the dumb kid who got left at the gas station? Luke could feel the back of his neck getting red, thinking about it. Careful not to look in that direction, he walked purposefully back to the parking lot as if he were out to stretch his legs.

"Melody? Chrissie? You two stay on the sidewalk or I'll make you sit in the car while I walk the dog," said a skinny woman in green shorts and a yellow T-shirt. She and two little girls were being pulled toward the dog-walking area by a panting boxer.

Luke gave them a wide berth and walked on slowly, sniffing the hamburger smells coming from the snack bar. He and Paul could have cooked hamburgers at the cottage tonight. He'd counted on being there by high tide, on jumping in the bay for a long swim. According to the tide chart that he'd kept taped inside his locker all year, the second high tide on the island today was at 6:55 P.M., which meant an easy hour on either side that was good for swimming. But now they'd never get there in time.

It wasn't as if his brother would miss him right away. Luke knew better. Right now Paul would be slouched in the front seat fiddling with the radio, switching it from one rock station to another, probably trying to figure out some way to study while he drove. When he finally got around to noticing that Luke was gone, he'd come roaring back—but when would that be? Two hours from now? Three?

How many times had he circled the parking lot? Eight? Ten? Luke jammed both hands in his jeans pockets and started around again. When he passed the snack bar, he hesitated.

Could he go in there and buy himself a hamburger? The snack bar looked crowded but maybe it was like the cafeteria at school where most people were waiting for special orders like onion rings and hot fudge sundaes, instead of things that were put together and ready so that you could just point at them. And he really was hungry. Luke swallowed and pushed the door open.

The loud music hit him first, jarring his senses. A tall man, leaving with a cardboard tray of milkshakes and burgers, jostled him. Four or five teenagers came in after him, talking and laughing, pushing Luke ahead of them toward the counter.

"What'll you have?" asked the sharp-voiced little waitress, hovering over her computer, ready to punch in his order.

Luke was conscious of the people behind him, waiting their turn. He heard the door open and other people come in. They were talking. Everyone in the snack bar seemed to be talking but all the words ran together like a foreign language. He could smell their sweat. He could smell hot oil, and french fries cooking, and coffee, but for a minute he couldn't remember why he was there.

"What do you want?" the woman demanded, sounding more tired than impatient.

The big, lighted menu sign behind her seemed to

Luke to grow brighter, bigger. But there was no food in sight—nothing to point at. Behind him, someone shuffled his feet impatiently. Luke opened his mouth, knowing ahead of time that it wouldn't work—aware already of the walls closing in on him as if he were on an elevator that was getting smaller and smaller. Straining, he fought to bring out the word, losing hope as he heard the strangled sounds coming from his throat. He gagged. His face burning like fire, he turned and pushed through the crowd, out the door.

Back on the hot tarmac, he gulped for breath. All right, he'd blown it. And it was his own fault. He'd broken his own first rule: Don't be conspicuous.

Still breathing hard, he left the walk and cut through the far side of the parking lot, heading down a row that was all big stuff like buses and trailers—things that gave some shade. Suddenly a white poodle darted out from under a bullet-shaped trailer and started toward him, growling.

"Beat it!" Luke whispered, and kept moving, careful not to step up his pace. The poodle followed, dancing circles around him, barking its fool head off.

"Shut up!" This was all he needed, Luke thought. The people in the snack bar must have figured him for a loony bird. Here among the trailers they'd take him for a burglar. "Quiet!" he hissed.

The poodle barked louder. Luke glanced around uneasily. He had to shut up the dog. "Grrrrr!" he went, growling back at it, raising his arms menacingly as he stomped toward it. *"Grrrrr!"*

The poodle backed off. It barked again, but doubtfully, and then moved away, shaken.

9

Luke walked on, feeling more in control. He'd done something, even if it wasn't earthshaking. Then, behind him, he heard a familiar sound, the funny panting noise the Volvo made at any speed under fifteen miles an hour.

Warily, Luke glanced over his shoulder. It was Paul.

"Get in!" he said in a grim voice, and leaned across the seat to open the car door.

CHAPTER THREE

LUKE'S legs felt wobbly, as though he'd been running for a long time. Awkwardly, trying not to step on all the books, he got in beside his brother and pulled the door closed. Without even looking at him, Paul sped along the access road, gunned the motor, and hurled them out into the traffic.

"Fasten your seat belt!" he said.

Luke sat bolt upright and fastened his seat belt. Paul was mad—and that wasn't fair. Paul had gone off and left him, not the other way round. Anyone in his right mind would have looked in the backseat before he drove off. Dad or Mom would have. For all Paul knew, Luke might have been strangled in his sleep. He could have driven off with a corpse in the car, and it would have served him right.

Luke studied his brother. How long was he going to act like this? Why didn't he say something?

Then Paul exploded. "Where the devil were you? How do you think I felt when I looked back and you weren't even there?"

Luke stared at him, incredulous. "How do you think *I* felt?" he yelled back. For a moment he hated

Paul. He wanted to pound him in the face with his fists. He wanted to make him understand how it felt to be left behind like an old comic book in a place that wasn't even a town—didn't even have a name.

Then he got ahold of himself. He unclenched his fists and took a deep breath. "I had to go to the bathroom," he said carefully, keeping his eyes fixed on the flapping mudguards of the truck ahead.

"Couldn't you wait for me to come back?"

"I guess I could have, but the lady from the Winnebago was sitting right there. I figured she'd keep an eye on our car."

"Did you ask her to?"

"No. And I wasn't *afraid* to talk to her," Luke said in a rush. "I just didn't want to. I should have locked the car, then you would have known I was gone. I'm sorry."

"You're *sorry*?" Paul pushed up his glasses and rubbed his eyes. He wasn't yelling anymore, and that made it worse. "I drove home last night after my last exam. I drove all day today while you slept, and I'm driving this stretch of highway for the third time in a row because you didn't have the nerve to ask a little old lady to tell me you'd be right back."

Luke's stomach lurched, the way it had at the airport after they'd dropped off the folks.

Then Paul reached over and mussed up Luke's hair. "I'm sorry, too, Luke. I should have checked in the backseat before I drove off." He slumped behind the wheel, his eyes on the road. "What are you going to do with yourself this summer? I'll be pretty busy, you know. A lot of reading to do and not much time to do it."

"I know that. I can take care of myself." All the same, he was aware of a pang of disappointment. Which was dumb. It was exactly what Paul had told the folks—that what he really had to do this summer was study and earn money. "I guess you're pretty tired of driving?"

"I'm all right. I just wish I didn't have to work first thing tomorrow morning. I promised Mr. Callaway that I'd help get the greens in shape before the tournament."

"When will we get there? Will there still be time for a swim?"

Paul checked his watch, then he leaned on the accelerator and passed a pickup truck full of chicken crates. "Probably not. We might have made it before we fouled up back there, but not now." He looked sideways at Luke. "Remember when you got kept after school the first day of first grade? Do you remember that day?

"Sort of," Luke said unwillingly.

"Mom made me go over to get you and I had to convince Mrs. Owens that you already knew how to read—that I'd taught you to read the summer you were four." Paul grinned and shook his head in disbelief. "You wouldn't tell her you could, you wouldn't read aloud to her, and you wouldn't give back your reader."

"She didn't bother me after that. None of the teachers did, much."

"Maybe someone should have, Luke." Paul glanced in the rearview mirror and changed lanes to pass a moving van. "You've always been shy, but I swear it's get-

13

ting worse instead of better. I've been away so much, I didn't realize you hadn't outgrown it.

"Last year, I honestly thought the folks were making a mountain out of a molehill, moving away from the island, I mean."

Luke stared at him, confused. He knew why they'd moved. Dad had finally finished his book. He needed to take a teaching job near a big library so he could do research for his next one. That's what they'd told him anyway.

Paul shook his head. "Now I'm beginning to think they were right."

"I don't know what you're talking about," Luke said loudly.

"Don't get riled up," Paul said with a grin. He tried the radio again. "Last summer you went for weeks on end without speaking to anyone except us—and Joanna Hill. I'm only saying that maybe the folks were right to move to Baltimore."

The words stunned Luke, but he believed them. Maybe he'd always known that losing the island was his own fault. All the same, if Mom and Dad had taken him away for his own sake, then they'd made a big, fat mistake.

And when they came home from Greece, he'd sure tell them how wrong they were. They could sell the house in Baltimore—give it away—and move back to the cottage where they belonged. And if they wouldn't do it, he'd come alone. He'd find a way to stay on the island by himself. He wasn't going through another year like the last one—dumped in a school so big that you needed a map to find your way to the lunchroom, where every sixth-grader was supposed to know how to use a computer in math, give book reports out loud, and climb a skinny little rope to the top of the gym in physical education.

"There's the boatyard," said Paul.

Luke sat forward, his muscles tense. He couldn't see the bay but he could almost smell it. Resolutely, he pushed what Paul had told him to the back of his mind. He couldn't think about it now. Now he had to pay attention. There was the old lighthouse . . . then the bridge loomed ahead of them, a thin high arch against the darkening sky. Paul was driving fast, whizzing past the people still fishing from the bridge, but Luke caught a glimpse of one small sailboat down on the water, its lights twinkling. Up they drove to the very top of the bridge. The tires buzzed and the Volvo shimmied from side to side on the corrugated surface. Then down the other side, and they were on the island at last.

CHAPTER FOUR

PAUL tossed the last suitcase out onto the moonlit grass and let the trunk fall closed. "Did you bring a flashlight?" he asked with a yawn.

"I can get the door open in the dark," Luke said. He knew every inch of the house and the yard. As often as he had dreamed of coming back, it had always been in the sunlight, but now the night smells, the soft noises and stirrings in the darkness seemed right. Methodically, he loaded himself up with the typewriter, the golf bag, his suitcase. Slow and easy. After months of waiting, it was important not to rush now. At a nod from Paul, he led the way across the silver grass to the big pine tree where it was black dark. Here he walked from memory, going around the bumpy roots and sunken spots so that Paul wouldn't trip. The dried pine needles were springy underfoot, and he could smell the tangled vines and brush that bordered the long backyard on both sides.

Once they were out from under the pine, he could see the gray shingled cottage. Its roof was tipped with light from the rising moon, but the rest was a dark mass. Next door, on the north side, the Hills' bungalow was dark, too.

16

Luke felt let down. Without even thinking about it, he'd counted on Joanna being here. In the past he'd been the one who waited. Every year Luke would begin to watch for Jo on the first hot day of the summer and go on watching until her family's overloaded station wagon finally turned into the lane.

"Why aren't the Hills here?" he asked.

"They're here—just out. When Dad talked to him on the phone, Mr. Hill said he'd open a few windows for us, but that they had to go somewhere to a wedding." Paul stopped. "He probably never thought to pull the power switch. We should have brought a flashlight."

"I can do that, too. I know where some candles are, and matches, and I've watched Dad—"

"Watch your head!" Paul warned too late.

Luke walked right into the overhanging porch roof and almost split his skull open. At least it felt that way, he thought, reeling. Now he knew what people meant when they talked about seeing stars—except what he saw were more like rings of white light circling his head.

"Are you all right?"

"Yes," said Luke. Very carefully he ducked under the low eave and set down his load. Must have grown some, he decided.

Dry leaves rustled as he opened the screen door— last fall's leaves that no one had swept away—and he felt for the keyhole. Paul was breathing down his neck when he unlocked the door and pushed it open.

"Cross your fingers," Paul said. He reached around to flip on the switch.

Harsh yellow light lit up the room. Luke followed

Paul into the small, dusty kitchen and looked with surprise at the cracks in the linoleum floor, the mouse droppings on the scarred wooden table, then at the rusty water that spurted into the sink when Paul turned on the faucet.

"Electricity's on, pump's running. Is the refrigerator plugged in, Luke?"

"No." The refrigerator wasn't even closed. Mom had taped a chock of wood in the door to let air in. But when Luke checked inside it was musty anyway—and empty. His stomach growled as he crawled behind the refrigerator to plug it in. The hum of electricity helped, but the kitchen didn't seem real without something cooking on the stove. And the dining room beyond was shadowy and smelled of bug bomb.

"It's pretty stuffy upstairs, too," said Paul, coming down the steps to find Luke standing unhappily in the middle of the living room.

"Did we bring anything to eat?" Luke asked.

"No. There're some cans of soup in the cupboard, but let's get moved in first. Let me see your head." Paul parted Luke's mop of hair. "A goose egg on the way but no skin broken. Does it hurt?"

"Only when you touch it." Luke broke away and made for the stairs.

"Take these up as you go," Paul said, pointing. "I'll bring the rest in from the car."

Luke carried the suitcases up the narrow stairs, staggering, and ran head on into a layer of hot air at the top. Stuffy? It was stifling! Hurriedly, he dumped one suitcase in Paul's room and took the other next door to his own. It was from his own room that he wanted to see the water again for the first time.

Framed in the center of his bedroom window, the long bridge sparkled exactly the way he remembered. Beneath it, tiny lights on invisible boats moved up and down the bay, and the moon made a track of brightness on the dark water. Drawn to the window like a magnet, Luke walked across the room, dropping his suitcase on the foot of his bed as he passed it.

A scurrying noise made him go back to turn on the light. Unnerved, he stared at the bed. At first, he thought someone had left something on it—some kind of plaster countryside with hills and valleys and roads, the sort of thing that people buy or build for model railroad trains. Then, advancing cautiously, he discovered the truth. His mattress had been invaded, moved into. Mice—a whole city of mice—had eaten a big, fuzzy-edged hole right smack in the center of his bed and then settled into it with all their living relatives. And, next to the hole were the chewed remnants of his copy of *The Jungle Book*.

Luke picked up the book, then dropped it in disgust. Last August his mom had gone all over the house, shutting all the paper towels and toilet paper into closed cupboards, putting the soap and candles, the matches, into glass jars so that the mice wouldn't eat them. So what had the mice eaten? His bed and his favorite book.

He should have known—should have expected it. Nothing had gone right all day.

Angry, he moved over to the window and took out the screen. He propped the window open, dragged the mattress off his bed, and started stuffing it out the opening. It wasn't easy, but he did it—jammed enough of it through so that he could shove the rest out and over the edge.

Then he opened his suitcase, changed to his swim trunks and a pair of old sneakers, and ran downstairs to tackle Paul.

"DON'T be stupid," said Paul tiredly. He was standing at the dining room window, staring out at the bridge. "You can't go swimming in the dark."

"It's almost a full moon."

"The tide's low. You'd have to walk way out."

Luke shook his head, grinning. "I'm shorter than you are. As soon as I get through the eel grass, I can start swimming." He looked at Paul hard. "The thing is, I really need to go swimming tonight."

Paul sighed. "It'll be cold," he said with a shudder.

Luke knew he'd won. "You don't have to come in. You can sit on the seawall and watch." Before Paul could think of more objections, he ran outside and jumped off the wall onto the pebbly beach.

"Five minutes tops!" Paul called after him.

"Right!" Luke wished he could just dive into the bay—that he didn't have to wade in inch by inch—but there was no other way to do it. He sucked in his breath and moved faster as the cold black water lapped over the tops of his tennis shoes and filled them. When the numbing, icy stuff was up to his knees, he opened his mouth wide in a soundless scream and splashed on as fast as he could until he was waist-deep in it. Then he stretched out his arms and threw himself face first into the water.

For a moment the shock paralyzed him, then he came up swimming in a flailing butterfly stroke. Faster and faster he swam, pumping himself warm again, licking the salt off his mouth, feeling strong enough to swim to the opposite shore.

"Sideways!" came Paul's warning over the water. "Don't go out any farther!"

Obediently, Luke flipped over on his back and swam parallel to the seawall, counting the stars, moving lazily now, closer and closer to the golden path of moonlight. He was whole again. Everything that had gone wrong during the day—during the whole year—was washed away by the cold, clean seawater. At this moment he felt as if he could do anything. It was like the scene in the movie when Superman got back his power by holding a glowing crystal prism in his cupped hands. The island gave him his power.

"Five minutes!" called Paul.

In one last burst of energy Luke shot forward into the band of reflected moonlight, shattering it into a million fragments. Then he turned and swam back to the eel grass. When he stood up to wade to shore, the air was warm. He could smell the chocolaty aroma of the privet hedge.

"How was it? Cold?" asked Paul from the seawall. His voice was easy now, relaxed.

"Nice," said Luke.

Then a car door slammed. They heard voices. Lights came on in the Hills' bungalow. Luke's eyes brightened. Maybe Joanna would break loose from her family and come look for him. She had to have seen the Volvo when they drove past. He waited, slapping at mosquitoes, but no one came out on the Hills' porch. Lights went on in their kitchen and through the open kitchen window he could hear the twins, Ed and Chris, arguing, and Rob chiming in.

Paul got to his feet and stretched. He jerked his head toward the bungalow. "Do you want to go say hello?"

Luke hesitated. What he wanted was for Jo to come outside. He could hear Mr. Hill's voice now, trying to settle the argument, and Mrs. Hill, trying to settle all of them. "I guess not," he said finally, and shivered.

"Then go get dry. I'll tell them we got here all right."

Luke ran up the steps and into the house. Upstairs, getting into his pajamas, he was mad at himself for not going to the Hills' back door to talk to Jo, but nothing could spoil the way he felt after his swim. With a contented smile, he put the screen back into the window and considered the bare bedsprings. He took the mattress from one of the cots in the extra bedroom and put it on his own springs. By the time he heard Paul coming up the stairs, his bed was made up and he was in it.

But why was he in it when he was hungry enough to eat a horse? And if Paul was coming to bed, too, then no one—

"Soup's on!" Paul called from the top of the stairs. He ducked under the door curtain into Luke's bedroom. "It isn't really soup. I just put what Mrs. Hill sent us into two bowls, and poured us some milk."

"Milk?" said Luke.

"She gave us a quart of milk, too."

"What else?" Luke asked, reaching for the big bowl

that Paul was carrying. Bread pudding! He set the tall glass of milk on the table beside his bed and picked up the spoon. Buttery, crusty-brown, moist bread pudding with raisins, he thought happily, eating mouthful after mouthful. All he needed to make things perfect!

Paul grinned at him and went to the door. "Oh, I almost forgot. Joanna sent you a message."

"What?"

"She said, 'Tell Luke we'll be over right after breakfast.' "

Luke almost choked. "Who's we?"

"How do I know? One of her brothers, maybe?"

Alex was almost as old as Paul and never around. The twins were eighteen. Even Rob, who was fourteen, only bothered with Luke and Jo when he was bored. "It can't be any of her brothers," he said after he swallowed.

"Well, you'll find out in the morning, I guess," Paul said, yawning. " 'Night, Luke."

CHAPTER FIVE

"HELP! *Shooo*-ooo! Beat it!"

After that there were some muddled, sputtery clucking sounds—enough so that Luke stirred without opening his eyes. Was he dreaming, or had his brother really called for help?

"Bring me the broom!" Paul bellowed.

Luke sat up, wide awake now. As fast as he could, he pulled on cutoffs and sneakers and ran downstairs. What he saw on the other side of the big screen doors stopped him in his tracks. Paul was under attack. Barefoot and still in his wet swim trunks, he was backed up against the weathered porch swing, trying to hold off a spread-winged, squawking rooster with the overturned lamp table.

"Hit him with the broom!" he yelled when he saw Luke coming.

"That's Pee Wee!" Luke said, shocked. Pee Wee was the meanest bird ever hatched, but Mrs. Bessemer had raised him from someone's abandoned Easter chick and she loved him.

"I *know* it's Pee Wee. Get him away or I'll kill him."

Paul was bleeding from a nick under the ribs where

Pee Wee had already connected, and he was mad as blazes. As the rooster tried for a flapping rush at his face, he raised the table high—then, when the thwarted bird dove for his ankles, he brought the table to the floor in what was almost a karate chop. Quickly, Luke grabbed the asbestos gloves that hung next to the fireplace and ran out on the porch.

"I thought you were at work," he yelled, pulling on the long, padded gloves. Pee Wee made as much noise as a barnyard full of chickens, so he had to shout.

"I'm finished," Paul yelled back. "I couldn't get to sleep last night. Whenever I closed my eyes, I was back behind the wheel driving again. Figured—with the full moon—I might as well go over to the club and do the mowing."

Luke grabbed for the big white rooster and got him. Pee Wee screeched but Luke held on, keeping the strong wings pinned close to the chicken's body the way Mrs. Bessemer did when she had to carry him. "I'll take him home and come right back for breakfast," he offered, going slowly down the porch steps.

"Don't hurry on my account. I'm going to bed," Paul said grimly. He picked a white feather off his wet arm and went into the house, letting the screen door slam.

"What about breakfast?"

"Open a can of soup."

Luke laughed, and got a better grip on the squirming rooster. Maybe he'd starve to death, but he was free. Sunrise had turned the calm, early-morning bay to liquid gold. Fishing boats moved across it silently, followed by trailers of gulls—each more raucous than Pee Wee.

Luke ran down the steps to the beach and out to the gleaming water. He'd been right last night. This was where he needed to be. If Mom and Dad wouldn't move back—if Mom had grown too used to drinking herb tea with the other sculptors who had studios near hers in the old Baltimore warehouse—if Dad couldn't bear to teach at the small college near the island again—then he would have to find a way to stay here without them.

He shook his head uncertainly and hurried along the rocky shore, walking just inside the rim of green seaweed that the tide had left. The openness of the sky and the water made him laugh, and he couldn't stop looking around him. Beyond the fishing boats, a gray navy training ship was dropping anchor. He and Jo had watched more anchors being dropped and pulled up again than most of the navy ensigns at the nearby base. Luke glanced over his shoulder, hoping to see her behind him, but there was no one on the beach.

Pee Wee jerked in his arms. Luke saw that they were at Mrs. Bessemer's low white house, and he left the rocky beach for the grass. When he was little, he'd been afraid to cross this long green lawn because the windows in the house seemed to stare back at him. Now he knew that Mrs. Bessemer was too busy to spy on people. He'd known she was all right ever since he and Jo had brought her a baby bird with a twisted leg. That sparrow still limped, but it was fine. Named Sally. More than likely, Sally and the Labrador, Charcoal, would answer the door with her.

Luke leaned on the doorbell with his elbow. He held Pee Wee out in front so that Mrs. Bessemer would see the rooster first. But when the door swung open, his grin disappeared.

"Hello, th-there!" said a man that Luke had never seen before. He had a bright red sunburn that looked as if it hurt, and he smiled when he saw Pee Wee. "You must want our local b-b-bird expert."

Luke stood there, dismayed. All he wanted to do was go, but the stranger made no move to take Pee Wee. Neither did Mrs. Bessemer when she saw him, but her pale blue eyes brightened as soon as she was close enough to recognize Luke. "Brought back the run-away for me again, did you? Next you can find Chark. He's gone off on his own, too," she said, as if Luke had never been away. She motioned behind her. "Pee Wee's nose is out of joint because Hector's here for a spell."

Luke glanced at the sea gull perched atop a plastic sheet on the high-backed couch, then he looked over his shoulder. Usually Hector dropped in when it was about to storm, but the sky was blue and cloudless.

Mrs. Bessemer knew what he was thinking. "No, it'll stay fair, I think. Hector's just come for rest and free feed. He's over twenty years old now, remember." She clucked reprovingly at Pee Wee. "Put that cock-of-the-walk out in his pen, will you, Luke? Otherwise, he'll keep on trying to rule the roost."

Luke nodded. He wanted to ask how Sally was, how long Chark had been gone, but he couldn't talk in front of the man with the sunburn. What was he doing here anyway? No one ever dropped in on Mrs. Besse-mer. That was something that Luke had been able to count on. She didn't like a lot of people around the place any more than he did. In fact, no one much but Luke and Joanna ever came inside the house. Or hadn't—until now.

"D-D-Do you th-th-think he's any b-b-better?"

Startled, Luke looked back at the two of them standing near the cage that Mrs. Bessemer kept for emergencies. What do you know? The guy was a stutterer. Not sure why that made him feel guilty, Luke carried the protesting Pee Wee through the neat, sparse kitchen. As they went past the bowls of mash and birdseed that were lined up on the kitchen counter, the rooster screeched and struggled in Luke's arms, trying to grab a bite. But when Luke got him out the back door and pushed him into his own section of the big, square pen, Pee Wee only hopped on his perch and began to preen himself.

"You're a bird all right," Luke said softly. He took off the gloves and turned to go back into the house. Then, out of the corner of his eye, he saw a slight movement at the farthest end of the enclosure. What kind of a bird was that? Not a bird—an animal. Was Mrs. Bessemer keeping a puppy in one of the ground-level pens?

He walked closer. It was a fox, a sleepy-looking little vixen, panting and blinking in the sunlight. Luke knelt in front of the cage, making coaxing noises, trying to get her to come to him. She didn't act wild. Certainly she wasn't afraid of him—wouldn't pay any attention to him. Why not? he wondered. Even if she were blind, she would smell him. Luke stood up. Maybe that guy was gone now, and he could ask Mrs. Bessemer about her.

But when he went inside, Mrs. Bessemer and the

stranger were still in the living room, over by the corner cage. Curious, Luke went closer to see what was in the cage.

"He found a baby swallow on the beach. Cat robbed the nest probably, then got scared off," Mrs. Bessemer said without turning. She straighened the flexible lamp wired to the top of the cage and rebent it to warm the damp hatchling from the other side. "But it won't eat," she went on, holding the flat stick above the tiny bird's head.

"Let me t-t-try," the young man said. "I didn't mean t-t-to make more work for you." He took the bowl and the flat stick from her, moistening his own mouth with the tip of his tongue as he tried to get the woebegone little bird to open its beak.

Luke was pretty sure it wasn't going to work. Not the way the tiny bird was hunched up. Besides, the goop on the stick looked like mashed-up Oreos, and Mrs. Bessemer only used cookies after they'd turned down good stuff like baby food and Cream of Wheat. Feeling sorry for both the guy and the bird, he moved toward the door.

"Wait!" the stranger called after him, and crossed the room in three strides. He held out his hand to Luke. "I'm Mike. Mrs. B-B-Bessemer says you've helped her with a lot of b-b-birds. D-D-Do you th-th-think th-th-this little fellow's g-g-got a chance?"

Luke's mouth turned as dry as a Popsicle stick. All he could think about was what had happened to him yesterday at the snack bar when he tried to order a hamburger. If he started choking and gagging now, this guy would think he was making fun of him. His face burning with embarrassment, Luke shrugged helplessly and reached for the man's outstretched hand. To his astonishment, it was bleeding.

"Whoops! Sorry about th-th-that," Mike said, trying to stick the loose end of the Band-Aid over the cut on his hand again. "T-T-Tangled with a lobster," he explained. With a cheerful grin, he backed off. "See you later, maybe?"

Luke nodded, and left in a hurry. Outside, the wind was up and the blue water was all ripples and little whitecaps.

"Hey, Luke?"

He swung around. It was Paul—standing out on the big rock.

"Breakfast's ready! Come and get it!"

Luke waved to show he'd heard and started running. He'd been pretty sure that Paul would change his mind and fix breakfast for them, and whatever it was, he was ready for it.

"WHAT is it?" he said three minutes later, poking at the sticky brown glob with his fork.

"Bean curd and brown rice." Paul plopped some on his own plate. "It's a recipe I used to make a lot at the apartment. I even made it for the folks once last summer. Maybe you were off somewhere with Joanna."

"Where did you get the stuff for it?"

"In the cupboard. I had a can of bean curd left over." Paul finished his plateful and rubbed his eyes sleepily. "Eat it, Luke. It's a lot better for you than a greasy hamburger," he added, and went upstairs to bed.

Luke sat there and thought longingly of greasy hamburgers. He wondered if the man who'd found the baby swallow lived close by. Maybe he'd see him on the beach sometime?

"Hey, Luke?"

Luke smiled. Finally, Joanna. He got up and dumped the stuff on his plate into the garbage pail. "Come on in!"

"Come on out! I want you to meet someone."

CHAPTER SIX

HE'D forgotten that Joanna wasn't going to be alone. Slowly, he walked into the dining room. Suppose it was her cousin Allie? Allie had spent two weeks with the Hills a few years back, and she'd been afraid of the water, afraid of the black snakes, afraid of the mice. He and Jo had had to take her with them everywhere, and she'd never once stopped talking. Don't let it be Allie, he prayed, and stepped out on the porch.

"Surprise!"

Luke was surprised, all right. Relieved, too. When the black puppy ran up and buried its teeth in his ankle, all he could do was laugh. Because it was about as different from Allie as you could get—all bite and no bark. "Whoa, boy!" he said, working his fingers between the tiny jaws, trying to pry the pup loose without hurting it. "He's something!" he said to Jo, grinning. "You ought to call him Jaws."

Joanna shook her head. "Bear—that's his name. Don't you think he looks like one?" She pulled the puppy away but it flew back at Luke's foot as if to a magnet, growling. "Hey," she said, "he really likes you."

Luke unfastened Bear from his sock. "What does he do if he doesn't like you?"

"I don't know." Her eyes laughed. "So far he's liked everyone." She dragged Bear off the porch by his leash. "Come on, let's take him for a walk."

Luke jumped off the seawall, then turned to watch Joanna lead the pup down the steps. Her hair was different, softer-looking. She was wearing white shorts and a white shirt, and she was longer-legged than she'd been last summer. In fact, she looked a lot like Melissa Eich, who'd been voted the prettiest girl in sixth grade. "How was school this year?" he asked.

"All right," she said, startled.

He realized that he'd never asked her that before. They'd always just picked up where they left off in the fall. He waited until she caught up with him, then he started walking into the wind. The water in the bay was all swirls now, and the puppy pranced ahead of them at the end of his leash.

"See?" said Jo proudly. "He does all right when he's going somewhere."

"What kind of a dog is he?"

"He's a Schipperke. It's Belgian or something for 'little skipper.' They were bred to ride the barges on the canals—to fight the rats off." Jo smiled. "Bear's a real fighter, too. Would you believe that Rob was afraid to go in the kitchen barefoot this morning because Bear was in there guarding the Hershey bar *he*'d left on the chair." She looked back over her shoulder. "There's Rob now. Come on!" she said, laughing, and took off.

Luke ran with her, for the sheer joy of running, knowing that Rob could never keep up with them. He hadn't run this course the way they had—day after day, summer after summer. They always lost him completely when they got to the big rocks, a long stretch of boulders each about three or four feet across with its own angles and holes and bumps, laid out one after another for what seemed like a quarter of a mile. But every rock was close enough to the next so that there was no reason to touch beach until you'd run the length of them.

With a whoop, Jo leapt up on the first rock and Luke and Bear sailed after her. Two long steps across, then a leap to the next, and the next and the next, all the way to the end with the timing, the pattern almost like a dance—the way it had to be. Laughing, they jumped off the huge last rock onto the pebbly shore.

Luke gazed at Joanna with satisfaction. She had a smudge on her chin, her shirt had come out of her belt, and she looked exactly the way she was supposed to look. And Rob was nowhere in sight.

"Left at the post. Eats too many Hershey bars," Jo said, gasping for breath.

Luke smiled and pulled the pup away from a dead fish. The rocky shoreline was almost deserted. Ahead of them, one lone fisherman walked along the edge of the water—a guy about Paul's age wearing cutoffs and sneakers, carrying a rod and a bucket of bait. Then, about midway between them and the fisherman, a black Labrador came out of the water and shook himself.

It was Chark—good old Chark—just coming in from his morning swim. Bear caught sight of the big dog and shot off like a rocket, yanking his leash right out of Jo's hand.

"Oh, no!" she yelled. "Help me catch him, Luke!"

Luke laughed. The worst thing that could happen to Bear was that the Labrador would decide he was too little to run around alone and take him to Mrs. Bessemer.

The fisherman coming toward them must have figured it the same way. At first he'd run toward the yapping puppy, but about fifty yards away he stopped and stood watching with a smile on his face.

It was Mike, the man who stuttered. Maybe he'd come to take Chark home? Luke slowed down.

"Here, Bear!" Jo called, but the pup was still going strong, closing in on the Labrador.

Chark's ears twitched. He raised his graying muzzle as if he had caught Bear's scent, but it didn't seem to worry him. Instead of standing up to check it out, he rolled over on his back and wriggled against the warm, smooth slate, looking as goofy as the giant pandas that Luke had seen lolling about in the zoo. How could Jo worry about that old softy?

"Luke!" she called. "Bear'll bite *him,* don't you see? Then Chark might get mad."

Luke caught up with the pup and lunged, but Bear dodged him and made a wide circle around the Labrador, still yapping frantically. He was so excited now he'd probably fasten onto Chark's nose like a snapping turtle. Luke shook his head in disgust and got serious. Out of the corner of his eye, he saw Mike closing in, too.

"Now!" Jo yelled.

She dived for the pup and missed, but Luke stomped on the leash and brought Bear up short. Then the little rascal bucked like a bronco and slipped right out of his collar.

"*No!*" Jo screamed.

Bear made right for old Charcoal but Mike got there first and made the interception, scooping up the pup and holding him high in the air.

"G–Gu–Gotcha!" he said, cradling Bear in the palm of his hand like a football and passing him over Chark's head to Luke. "But th–th–this old fellow wouldn't hurt a puppy." Mike reached out to pet Chark. "You're a g–g–good b–b–boy, aren't you, mister?"

That was a mistake. He couldn't know Chark very well or he would never have been that friendly. Luke backed out of the way as Chark staggered to his feet, planted both paws on Mike's sunburned shoulders, and gave him a thorough wash job—face, hands, and chest.

"Whoa! No! D–D–Down, b–b–boy!"

Luke knew that Chark's claws on that raw skin must have hurt like crazy, but Mike kept his voice low and easy while he lifted the Lab's front paws off his shoulders. "G–G–Good b–b–boy. Stay d–d–down, b–b–boy," he said matter-of-factly.

Luke handed the squirming puppy to Jo, amazed that Mike could stutter so much and still seem so relaxed.

"Enough!" Mike said, laughing. He ducked away from the Labrador and picked up his fishing rod. Yawning hugely, Chark collapsed on the beach and closed his eyes.

"Thanks!" shouted Jo, who had moved on a hundred feet or so with the bright-eyed puppy.

"No p–p–problem," Mike said. He picked up his bucket of bait. "Th–That's a nice little Schipperke you've g–g–got th–th–there," he added, smiling. Then he nodded to Luke and started up the beach, splashing through the surf like a little kid.

Luke felt a sudden sense of loss. He should have at least tried to talk to the guy.

"Come on! Let's get away from here so I can put Bear down," Jo called to him.

Chark was snoring, his gleaming black belly rising and falling with his steady breathing. Luke smiled and ran to catch up with Joanna, setting a gull in flight as he passed the Martins' pier.

Jo waited until he got close, then she raced away with Bear at her heels. They ran as hard as they could run along the narrow strip of rocky beach—up one side of Gary Tartaglino's jetty and down the other, across the long, level stretch of blue-black slate in front of the Seabecks' house—until suddenly, with a sinking feeling, Luke saw three familiar-looking figures coming toward them. Jo must have recognized them as soon as he did because both of them stopped at the exact same time.

"Mrs. Rucklehaus," Jo said with a groan, unwinding Bear's leash from around her ankles. "*And* Mrs. O'Reilly. How can the Monsignor stand them?"

Luke knew what she meant. It was one of those times when he wished he were invisible. The Monsignor—still thin as a skeleton but with a quiet smile on his craggy face—only spoke when he had something to say; it was the other two you had to watch out for.

"Hello, Joanna!" called Mrs. Rucklehaus, bearing down on them with a broad smile. "How's your mother? Hello, Luke," she went on without giving Jo time to answer. "What's this I hear about your folks not even coming back for the summer? I knew how it would

be once they got to the big city. No time for old friends."
She shook her head and went on briskly. "Exactly what
I was talking about. The summer festival is a week from
this Saturday—the earliest we've ever had it—and
there's simply more work to be done than there are
people to do it. Why, we've already got the lobster meat
picked over and in the freezer, and we just dug the clams
for the fritters ourselves." She paused long enough to
gesture toward the Monsignor with his rusty black trou-
sers rolled up to his knees. Then she noticed Bear sniffing the wet burlap bag and gave Mrs. O'Reilly a
reproving look.

"Shooo!" said Mrs. O'Reilly, and poked at Bear
with her clam rake. The Monsignor squatted to pet the
pup, and Bear went right for his bony ankles.

Luke pulled Bear away and drifted down to the
water's edge. Not even Jo could get them out of this.
Mrs. Rucklehaus had roped them in last year, too. As
long as no one tried to make him work at the festival
itself, Luke didn't much care.

"So what day can you and Luke come help build
the craft tables?"

Before Jo could speak, Mrs. O'Reilly had whipped
a little notebook out of the pocket of her wet denim
skirt. "Let's see now," she said, turning pages. "How
about Saturday? Saturdays everybody either wants to
sleep late or take their boat out. We haven't nearly
enough people then."

"We haven't?" said Mrs. Rucklehaus. She smiled
brightly at Joanna. "Well then, Saturday it is—bright
and early. Oh, and tell your mother we're counting on

her to sell the used books again this year. I looked for her after ten o'clock mass but—"

"We went yesterday," Jo interrupted.

"We'll see you two on Saturday then," the Monsignor said, not bothering to hide his teasing grin. He picked up the bag of clams and started walking. The two women hurried after him, both talking at the same time.

Jo started running again and Luke ran after her. They didn't slow down until they got to Mrs. Bessemer's, where a man in a dark green uniform was coming out of the house with one of those animal carrier boxes.

"That's the game warden," said Jo, panting. "What do you think he's got in the cage?"

"The fox, probably," said Luke, and told her about the sleepy-looking little vixen that he'd seen in Mrs. Bessemer's backyard. "But I don't know why he would come get it on a Sunday."

"What was it doing there? Didn't you ask her?"

"She had company."

"Let's ask her now," Jo urged, her eyes bright with curiosity. "Maybe it wasn't the fox. If it's still there, I'd love to see it!" Then she hesitated. "Except it's almost lunchtime. Want to make sandwiches and eat them out on the big rock?"

Suddenly Luke was almost panicky hungry. He nodded and started running again, remembering last night's bread pudding. Maybe there was some of that left in the Hills' refrigerator?

CHAPTER SEVEN

OFTEN, in the next few days, Luke thought about stopping by Mrs. Bessemer's but things kept getting in the way.

Like Jo's teeth. Monday he had to ride over to the mainland to keep Bear company while Jo got her teeth cleaned. Jo refused to leave the puppy behind, and Mrs. Hill said *she* wasn't going to sit out in the car with him and be chewed alive.

Tuesday his brother left him a note telling him to trim the hedge and mow the lawn, which was like a jungle. The only good thing about Tuesday was that Paul brought home two New York strip steaks for their supper.

The next day Luke saw the notice on the library bulletin board:

LOST DOG

BLACK LABRADOR.
PLEASE RETURN TO
FOURTH HOUSE PAST BRIDGE
ON SHORE ROAD.
Reward!

"Hey, Jo," he whispered. "Look at this."

She read it over his shoulder. "That's got to be Chark."

Luke knew that. But it didn't make sense. Mrs. Bessemer *had* said something about Chark being missing, but they'd run into him on the beach after that. "We just saw Chark on Sunday."

"Today's Wednesday. That's three days ago, Luke," said Jo, sounding bored. "I worry about Bear if I haven't seen him for three minutes."

"Chark's different. He wanders all over the island."

"Maybe he's wandered home by now." She brightened. "Did you ever go see if the fox was still there?"

Luke shook his head.

"Do it now, then! I'll take Bear home first and ask Mom to watch him so he won't bite the fox."

"I SAW a notice at the library about a lost dog," Luke said, unsure of how to begin.

Mrs. Bessemer nodded.

"I thought Chark had come home," Luke said, watching as she stirred a drop of paregoric into baby cereal. "Right after you told me he was missing, Jo and I saw him on the beach."

"Are you sure it was Chark?" she asked quickly.

"Yes," said Luke. There were other Labradors that roamed the beach, but they were livelier dogs. Chark was lazy and gentle. "When did you see him last?"

"Last Friday." She handed Luke the cup and a flat stick, and went to open the door for Hector, who had been standing before it, waiting. "He came home for supper about six, the way he always does, but he wouldn't eat. He kept wanting me to pet him but he wouldn't touch his food. Then, when I let Hector out, Chark went, too." Her eyes held Luke's. "Did he seem all right when you saw him?"

"He was fine. He'd had a swim and was settling down for a nap."

Mrs. Bessemer opened the baby swallow's cage and motioned to him. Luke saw with surprise that he was still holding the cup and the stick—and that Mike's swallow had fluffed out some.

"What's his name?" he asked, offering a bit of cereal to the tiny bird.

"Pete. I had to feed him with an eyedropper until yesterday," said Mrs. Bessemer absently. "I can't get over the notion that Chark might have caught something from that sick fox. He kept nosing and nuzzling her until I put her in the cage."

"Is the fox still here?"

"No. I called Liz Gray at the library and she sent the animal control man to pick her up."

Luke wasn't having any luck getting Pete to open his beak, so he gave the cup and stick back to Mrs. Bessemer. "Where did she come from?" he asked, meaning the fox.

"Chark brought her."

"Chark?"

Mrs. Bessemer stroked the swallow's throat very gently with the side of her little finger. "He carried a kitten home in his mouth last winter. I don't know what he thought *that* was going to grow up to be." She shook her head. "The ultimate protector, that's Chark. Thinks that if anything needs taking care of, he's the one to do it." The baby swallow's beak opened. She got a bit of cereal in it, then looked at Luke. "What time of day did you see him?"

Time was always mixed up for Luke on the island. Sometimes, when he and Jo ambled along the beach for a few minutes, it was only a few minutes; other times it turned out to be two or three hours. But the Monsignor had been at ten o'clock mass and had almost certainly eaten lunch before he went clamming. "It was probably about one or two," Luke said finally. Then he added, "Jo'll be along. Maybe we'll go look for Chark?"

"I'd appreciate it," said Mrs. Bessemer. "But don't put yourselves out."

Luke shrugged. He could tell she was only pretending not to be worried. "Nothing else to do," he said, nonchalant. "Jo's probably waiting outside."

EXCEPT that she wasn't.

Luke crawled out on the big rock to see if she and Bear were hiding on the ledge just to be funny. He even knocked on the Hills' back door, but no one answered. When he discovered that their car was gone from the back lane, he gave up and walked along the shoreline to the stretch of beach where Bear had tried to take on the Labrador.

Common sense told him he wouldn't find Chark there, but still he was disappointed. Then he realized that he'd been expecting to see Mike as well.

Maybe there was a connection? Mike had petted

43

Chark, and he was a sociable dog. Suppose he'd decided to go fishing with Mike instead of taking a nap?

On impulse, Luke turned and walked north—the way Mike had gone—waving when he went by Mrs. Bessemer's in case she happened to be looking out the window. As he passed the pink bungalow, he saw that the Hills were still gone. But this time he noticed that the porch light was on. Mrs. Hill never did that unless they planned to come back after dark. Once he was past the point, a sea gull—maybe Hector—flew over him low and steady for a bit, then swerved inland and came down on the Binghams' garage roof.

The eastern shore of the island, especially the upper portion, was less built up than the rest. Luke walked for close to four hours—to the northern tip and back again—and saw almost no one. In what had always been the Schaffners' yard, a family he had never laid eyes on were having a cookout. The smell of it made his mouth water, and he hurried past. When he got home, he went straight to Mrs. Bessemer's.

She was out back giving Pee Wee his supper and putting seed in the open feeders. "For the transients," she always said.

"You didn't find him?" she said now, barely looking at Luke.

"No."

"Well, don't worry about it." This time she managed a smile. "The old layabout's just having a holiday. He'll come back when he's good and ready. Thank you very much for looking."

Luke hesitated, then started for the gate.

"Luke?"

He turned.

"It's nice to have you back."

He ran for it. How could she say that when he hadn't done any good at all? The island wasn't so big. He ought to be able to find Chark if he put his mind to it. If it wasn't dark after he ate something, he'd really start looking.

He ran up the porch steps and inside, remembering at the very last moment not to call out to his mother that he was home—remembering with the letdown feeling that had been with him all week that Paul was the only one here and that he might be sleeping.

But Paul was gone. A note on the refrigerator door said:

Forgot to mention that lawn looks much better. Will try today to get you a job helping Charlie in the Pro Shop. That way we can both buy our greasy hamburgers at employee rates (since we can't afford steaks all the time). Sounds good, huh?

Paul

It didn't sound good. In fact, it was about the dumbest idea Paul had ever had. He ought to know how Luke would feel. He probably thought the job would be good for him—like he thought Mom and Dad had been right to take Luke away from the island.

Luke wadded up the note and threw it in the trash. One time Pee Wee had been left out in his cage during a hailstorm. Mrs. Bessemer had said that when she finally remembered to bring him inside, he was so mad

45

he couldn't see straight. That was the way Luke felt now, bumping into the table as he crossed the kitchen. Paul had no right to line up a job for him without asking. Why had he gone back to work again, anyway? He hadn't had time to sleep—hadn't had time to do anything.

Then he stumbled over the mattress. It stood, folded over, just inside the dining room with the chewed book and yet another note from Paul on top. This one read simply:

Trash? Or did you drop something?

His face burning like fire, Luke shoved the remains of *The Jungle Book* into the bottom shelf of the bookcase behind a row of other books. Then he dragged the mattress out the back door and up to the end of the yard for Island Trash to take away.

He ought to have done it days ago, but he'd forgotten—forgotten that he'd even thrown the stupid mattress out the window. Luke slapped the dust off his hands angrily. In the time it took him to haul the dumb mattress into the house, Paul could have dragged it up to the road himself.

He opened the refrigerator and then slammed it in disgust. At least Paul could have bought some groceries. What did he mean to do? Buy one meal at a time all summer?

Luke went to the cupboard. Wonderful! What a choice! Two cans of onion soup, leftover oyster crackers in a jelly jar, pancake syrup, and peanut butter.

He put the peanut butter and crackers on the kitchen table, got a glass of water, and settled down to some serious eating. Half a jar of peanut butter later, he felt better but sleepy. Yawning, he rescued *The Jungle Book* from the bookcase and went upstairs.

He'd been dumb, to be cross with Paul. The thing to do was wait up for him and say flat out that he wasn't going to take the job at the country club. And maybe he could find out if Paul had some kind of schedule. The way it had been so far, he never knew when his brother was going to be at work and when he wasn't. Maybe Paul could help him find Chark?

Luke punched up his pillow and stretched out on the bed to read and wait.

CHAPTER EIGHT

SUN shining in his face woke him, which meant he'd slept later than he usually did. Why hadn't Mom called him when she came up to her studio?

Then he remembered. He felt the stillness of the cottage, the emptiness. He listened. Sometimes Paul clattered his coffee cup on the table when he was studying, or snored if he wasn't. But this morning there was nothing. Maybe Paul hadn't even come home last night? Quickly Luke dressed and went next door to his brother's room.

Gone again. But he'd been here. The textbooks were stacked in a different order.

Luke ran downstairs and into the deserted kitchen. Without hope he opened the refrigerator. A pizza? Almost holding his breath, he slid the flat square cardboard box out of the refrigerator and raised the lid. Half a pizza, anyway, and with green peppers and sausage. He tore loose the first limp triangle and ate it standing up. Then he sat down at the table and polished off the other three. With a sigh of satisfaction, he stuffed the cardboard box into the trash.

CHARK hadn't come home when he checked with Mrs. Bessemer. The Hills' car was back and the porch light was off. Luke walked around the pink bungalow a couple of times, hoping that Bear would see him through one of the screens and bark.

The tide was too low to swim—even if he wanted to break the rules—so he waded out to the rocks where his mother had found an underwater garden of weird and bright-colored seaweeds. He poked around awhile but the water was murky. After a bit he smashed a mussel with a rock and dropped it into a shallow tidepool. Crouching there, watching the hermit crabs gather to fight over the mussel's bright orange flesh, he remembered the marsh on the other side of the island. Could Chark have gone over to the marsh?

Luke left in a hurry, glad to have a plan. He hated the traffic noises on the highway. As soon as he could, he turned off onto the shady dirt road that went past the Donnegals' horse farm and the old windmill. When he got to the marsh, he skirted the edges, scaring up frogs and startling the egrets that had come to feed on them. Mosquitoes bit him and gnats got in his eyes and up his nose. He slapped at them and spit them out. He walked with his eyes squinted, but kept walking through the high green grass with his sneakers making sucking sounds. Secretly, he was sort of proud of himself. Intrepid, that was the word. Once he stepped into the dirty water right up to his thighs. Twice he lost a shoe and had to feel around in the mud for it. When he'd gone full circle and was out on the road again, he saw the old man sitting on an overturned barrel in front of the bait shed.

Unhappily, Luke came to a stop. He ought to go ask him if he'd seen a black Labrador near the marsh. The old man always sat there, always looked like he hated the world. Probably he wouldn't answer. Anyway, why would Chark come here when he could swim in the bay? Luke ducked his head. Ashamed of himself for not asking, he turned and went home.

JOANNA was in her swimsuit, sitting out on the big rock. Bear jumped up on Luke, and Jo's eyes were bright with excitement. "Did you hear what happened?" she began, then stared at Luke's legs. "Where did you get so mucky?"

"Over at the marsh, looking for Chark. Where did you go?"

"My father decided to pack everyone in the car—after a three-minute warning—and drive to Vermont to visit his sister." She made a face. "I guess that means Chark didn't come home. Did you hear that they sent the fox to the mainland?"

"Why?"

"Because she died, and they want to find out why. Don't you want to go swimming? I'll wait for you while you put on your suit."

"All right." He did want to go swimming. More important, he needed a minute alone to think.

From habit he went to the kitchen first. A note on the refrigerator said:

> Where *do you go? Came back to get you so you could start job at club, but couldn't wait. Work late tonight. We'll talk tomorrow.*
> *Paul*

50

Luke opened the refrigerator to see if another pizza had materialized, but the shelves were bare. Too hot and sweaty to care, he went upstairs to change—and to think.

Mrs. Bessemer had been afraid that Chark might have caught something from the fox. Now the fox was dead, and all Luke could remember about her was that she'd been sleepy. Chark was almost always sleepy, so—Wait a minute, now. . . . There *was* something that made animals look sleepy. The skinny kid that everyone called Hobo had given a report about it in science class last year. It was rabies.

Luke pulled on his trunks, put his swim shoes on again, and hurried back outside. Bear, yapping excitedly, was tied to the handle of the lawn mower. Mr. Hill was putting hamburgers on the barbecue grill, and Jo was already in the water. Luke waded a few yards, then, glad the tide was higher, plunged in and swam out to her.

"The fox—" he said, treading water. "What did they think might be wrong with her? Was it rabies?"

"Don't be silly! There's never been any rabies on the island."

"There is in Maryland—an epidemic. Mostly raccoons, but other animals, too. They've had so many cases that people have to get shots for their cats as well as their dogs." He swam in a wide circle, trying to make sense of it. Sure, there'd never been any rabies on the island—but there were bridges, weren't there? And cars going back and forth all day long. Cars from all over. Cars with pets in them.

He dove under and came up in front of Jo. "Did

anyone say what they were worried about when they sent her away to be tested?"

"Nope." Jo tossed the wet hair out of her face and turned over to float on her back. "Mrs. O'Reilly called Mom about something and then said that the game warden and Doc Schaffner and Dr. Wainwright had a meeting and decided to do it. Anyway, you saw the fox. Was she frothing at the mouth?"

"No," said Luke. Hobo had talked about nocturnal animals wandering around in broad daylight and wild animals that acted tame, but he hadn't mentioned anything about that. "Maybe rabid animals don't really foam at the mouth—or don't always."

"Come and get it!" Mr. Hill called, waving to them with a paper plate.

"You, too!" Jo said quickly. When Luke hesitated, she went on. "Mom *said*. This is the last week of my Dad's vacation. From now on he can only come here weekends, so we won't have as many cookouts. Come on!"

They raced back to shore. For a change, Jo's oldest brother, Alex, was there, too, with his girlfriend from town, Alicia Barnes. Other summers Luke had come to these cookouts already fed—come mostly because Jo wanted him to—and they had taken their hamburgers over to the big rock. Tonight, along with the platter of hot dogs and hamburgers on buns and the tossed salad that Mrs. Hill always fixed, there was a big steamer of corn on the cob.

Too hungry to walk away from any of it, Luke heaped his plate with food, smiling when the butter ran off his corn and down his chin. The twins came and went almost before he noticed. Alex and Alicia moved over to sit on the rock, and even Rob minded his own business and ate.

Afterward, Luke and Jo went for a last walk on the beach with the sleepy puppy. When they came back, Mrs. Bessemer's house had only one faint light upstairs. She'd said that Chark would come home when he was ready, but Luke was beginning to think that wouldn't happen. He had to talk to Paul about it first thing in the morning. Because of the fox.

CHAPTER NINE

AT first Paul couldn't seem to understand why it was important.

"Let me get this straight," he said groggily. He sat up in bed, knocking a sheaf of papers off the end table. "The fox that Mrs. Bessemer was keeping died, and they took it to the mainland hospital to find out why. Right?"

"Right!" said Luke, trying to be patient.

"And *you* think it died of rabies?"

"Right! You see, this kid called Hobo gave a report about rabies in science class, and sleepy-looking was one of the symptoms he mentioned. The fox looked really sleepy, and the animal warden was worried enough to send her off for testing, so I figured—"

"Hold on!" Paul waved for him to stop. "Don't tell me that part again. Just explain where Chark comes into it."

"Well, Chark always looks sleepy, but Mrs. Bessemer says he'd been nuzzling the fox before it died— and now she doesn't know where he is. So if the fox *is* rabid, Chark may be sick, too, don't you see? We've got to find him and take him to Doc. Maybe there's something Doc can do."

Paul leaned back against his pillow and closed his eyes. "You don't get rabies out of the air, Luke. Has Chark bitten anyone?"

"Of course not."

"Then find him so you can stop worrying. Eat some breakfast and go look for the dog!"

"There isn't any breakfast." Before Paul had time to interrupt, Luke went on quickly. "And don't say, 'Open a can of soup,' because it's onion."

Paul rubbed his eyes sleepily. "Sorry. The store was closed when I left work. After this week I'll only be working thirty hours." He looked at his watch. "If you can hold out a bit, I'll buy you a bang-up breakfast at the club before you start work." He suddenly looked pleased with himself. "Charlie says it'll have to be an informal arrangement because you're underage, but he can use the help."

"I don't want the job."

"What do you mean, you don't want the job?" Paul sat up, startled. "Look, Luke, you can't go through life hiding your head in the sand. Push yourself a little this summer. Get out and talk to people—work in the pro shop—and it'll be that much easier when you go back to Baltimore."

"Who said I was going back?"

"Of all the asinine—" Paul threw back the covers and got up. Then he sat back down on the edge of the bed. "Look, if you'd just try the job for a couple of days—"

"No."

"You're afraid to try it, aren't you?" Paul's voice rose in anger. "Afraid to sell golf tees and sun visors to a bunch of ordinary, pleasant men and women who've known you since you were born!"

"You—you—you're too skinny!" Luke said, pushing the words through his teeth so that Paul couldn't tell he was about to fall apart. He took a deep breath and made himself pretend to look critically at his brother's ribs and his hairy, bony legs. "You're probably starving. Give *me* the money and I'll buy some food."

Paul was mad enough to spit nails. He didn't even know he'd gotten to Luke first. All he did was march over to the dresser and take a twenty out of his billfold.

"Here! There's more household money if you need it—but I don't know what good it will do you. You don't have enough nerve to walk into Larsen's and buy a loaf of bread. What are you going to do? Give Mrs. Hill your shopping list?"

Luke wanted to jam the twenty in Paul's teeth. Instead, he put it in the zippered pocket of his shorts and went to his own room, to grab a knapsack. He'd show Paul. The trick was to stay mad.

He ran downstairs and outside. He wouldn't take his bike. He'd walk, so he could carry more—the knapsack on his back and another bag in his arms. How many bags could you buy for a twenty?

"Hey, Luke?"

It was Joanna. "I have to go to town with Mom," she called. "Want to come along for the ride?"

"No, thanks," Luke answered, without turning. Paul's words still stung. He had to get the groceries by himself. He didn't want any help. He waved half-heartedly and hurried the other way—down the beach. She'd think he was going to check on Chark. He would, too— on the off-chance that the Labrador had come home.

At Mrs. Bessemer's he rapped impatiently on the door.

"Why, Luke . . . the very person we need," said the dark-haired young woman.

Luke was fed up with other people opening Mrs. Bessemer's door. What was Mrs. Gray doing here?

"I'm driving Mrs. Bessemer to the hospital on the mainland," she said, as if he'd asked out loud. "Dr. Wainwright doesn't have the vaccine, and she has to get started on a series of anti-rabies shots. That fox she was taking care of turned out to be rabid." She looked at Luke closely. "Did you or Joanna go near it?"

He shook his head, stunned to find out he'd been right—ashamed of the fleeting sense of satisfaction that it gave him.

"Good. In any case, Mrs. Bessemer may as well stay with my sister until she gets the next shot at least, which means she'll need someone to—"

"Is that you, Luke?" With the unfamiliar black hat mashing down her hair, Mrs. Bessemer was a stranger. She seemed dazed at first, as if she'd forgotten what she was going to say, then she got hold of herself.

"Luke, will you take care of the birds for me until Tuesday—possibly Wednesday? Hector's outside, but the others are all in their cages. I've just fed the baby swallow and he should be all right until this afternoon. Give him Cream of Wheat and strained apricots. No more paregoric. And, Luke?"

He waited, uncertain.

"The animal control people are trying to find Chark now." She turned away and picked up her black suitcase. "Don't you go looking for him anymore, Luke. Don't go near him if he comes back."

"But—"

"It's my fault," Mrs. Bessemer went on apologetically. "Chark and I—we just took care of the birds. I never thought he might need taking care of. Never kept up his shots, you see?" She stepped out on the stoop. "That's why Dr. Schaffner says it's too late to help him—that is, if he did get rabies from the fox."

Luke's eyes widened.

"He says we'll know soon, but you stay away from Chark until we do. Understand?"

"We ought to go now," said Mrs. Gray.

Mrs. Bessemer handed Luke the door key. Then, all of a sudden, she looked stricken. "I forgot. The apricots are all gone. I finished the jar this morning." She opened her black pocketbook and gave Luke a dollar. "Do you mind buying another?"

Luke wanted to say that it was no problem, that he was going to the store anyway, but all he did was nod.

Mrs. Gray looked to make sure that Luke was still holding the key, then closed the door. "We can drop you in town if you want to pick up the apricots now," she said matter-of-factly, and Luke found himself walking up to the lane with them and sliding into the backseat of Mrs. Gray's Chevette.

The two women carried on a conversation of sorts in front, but all Luke could think about was Chark. Chark with Sally the sparrow taking a nap between his

58

big clumsy paws. Chark backing away, embarrassed—ducking his head—while Pee Wee pecked at him and heckled him and snatched hunks out of his fur, all because Mrs. Bessemer had taught him never to turn on a bird.

When the car stopped, Luke got out with his knapsack and stood there awkwardly.

"Don't let Joey and Sally out of the cage if you'd rather not," said Mrs. Bessemer.

Mrs. Gray drove away, and Luke walked blindly into the store. Not until he'd bumped into the row of wire grocery carts did he focus on the fact that he wasn't at Larsen's, the store where his mother had always shopped. This was the new market just off the highway.

Was that better, or worse? Better probably, he decided, and yanked one of the carts loose. No wisecracking Mr. Larsen behind the meat counter—no nosy Mrs. Larsen, who seemed to think he was retarded, waiting to be nice to him at the cash register.

He moved along pretty fast, remembering what his mother had said once about being afraid to shop before dinner because everything looked good to her when she was hungry. Before breakfast was worse. Luke grabbed a box of cinnamon doughnuts, checked the price, then put it back on the shelf.

Everything cost a lot more than he'd expected. After he found a couple of jars of strained apricots in the baby-food section, he moved up and down the aisles at a slower pace, figuring out roughly what he was spending as he tossed stuff into the cart—milk, cheese slices, margarine, bread, eggs, cereal, orange juice, and potato chips. Nothing but basics.

He added up the prices again, shook his head in disbelief, and pushed the cart around for a bit, just looking. Finally, he threw in a package of hot dogs, a whole chicken, a pound of hamburger meat, and a bag of rice. Then he took a long, hard look at what was in the cart and went back for the box of cinnamon doughnuts.

At the checkout counter he held his breath while a gum-chewing woman in a purple smock rang up his order. As she shoved each item past him, Luke added things up in his head one more time. When the woman got to the potato chips and doughnuts, which were last, Luke's mental calculator had already hit $19.00.

He broke out in a sweat. No way would he call Paul. In his mind was the blurred memory of his mother once not having enough money with her in a grocery store in Baltimore. What had she done? Put something back? Then he remembered the dollar that Mrs. Bessemer had given him.

The cash register tape shot out of the machine— total $20.87.

The woman smacked her chewing gum. Luke paid and left.

Outside the store, he took things out of the paper bags and packed them into the knapsack. Not everything fit, but then he saw Jo and Bear.

"In town alone?" she asked, looking surprised.

Luke nodded, a doughnut in his mouth. He offered her the box, and squirmed into the knapsack.

"Thanks," she said, helping herself. "Mom's collecting books for the summer festival, but we'll have to go home soon for lunch. Don't you want to wait for a ride?"

Luke shook his head and jammed another doughnut in his mouth. Then he took it out again and told Jo about the fox being rabid and Mrs. Gray taking Mrs. Bessemer to the mainland to get rabies shots.

"For heaven's sake!" said Jo, her eyes shining. "You were right after all. Hey? Are you going back the shore way?"

"Yes."

"Bear needs a walk." She pointed at the yellow house across the street. "Wait until I run into Mrs. O'Reilly's and tell Mom, and I'll go with you."

"Sure." He didn't mind waiting, because he'd done it. Maybe he'd cheated, not going to Larsen's, but he had the food, didn't he? When Paul came home tonight—whether he'd eaten at the club or not—there would be something in the dumb, empty refrigerator. Cooked food. The chicken could stew in a big pot of water with some rice while he was over at Mrs. Bessemer's.

"All set," Jo said. "I think she's glad to be rid of me. She brought me to help carry boxes, but I'm not much use with Bear along."

"Why didn't you leave him at home?"

"Can't. He eats things. This morning he ate a tennis racket, and yesterday, when we shut him in the back bedroom, he ate through the wall-to-wall carpet. Alex calls him Termite." She pointed. "Look at that police car, Luke!"

The black-and-white squad car went past the wharf, then right off the road onto the sandy beach, weaving its way among the picnickers and the people dragging their little sailboats from the road to the water's edge.

"There's some sort of commotion up the beach," Luke said, stuffing another doughnut in his mouth and giving the last one to Jo. "Come on!"

They couldn't run very fast. The grocery bag was a nuisance, and the knapsack bumped Luke's back, but the real trouble was that everyone in the harbor area was running in the same direction after the police car—kids on bikes, clammers carrying their rakes. Even when Jo and Luke got close, it was hard to see what was happening. The police car had stopped near the edge of the sandy beach, and there was a state policeman holding the crowd back.

"What's going on?" Jo asked, pulling his sleeve.

The trooper ignored her, but the man beside him turned around. "They found a dead dog in the brush above the shoreline."

"What kind of dog?" Jo asked, quickly picking up Bear.

"Someone said it was a Labrador."

"Stay back, folks!" The trooper called out.

Luke signaled Jo to wait for him; then he began to skirt the crowd. Once on the opposite side of the brush—the road side—he worked his way up the embankment through a tangle of weeds and Queen Anne's lace until he got to the top. In the clearing below lay a dead dog with a sleek black coat and a gently rounded belly.

It was Chark all right. Using a long-handled tool of some kind, a second policeman dragged the dog's body onto a heavy piece of sailcloth and made a rough package of it, tied with rope. When the package was knotted, the trooper dragged it down to the beach.

"Stand back now," the first trooper was saying when Luke got back to Joanna. "It's only a dead dog, folks. No cause for alarm. We've had a case of rabies reported, so all animal carcasses have to be sent to the mainland for testing. Back away while we get this into the trunk of the cruiser."

"It doesn't have to be Chark," Jo whispered.

"It is, though," Luke said. Then he pointed to the sea gull circling overhead. "And Hector's probably the one that found him." He felt like throwing up. If he'd brought Chark home that Sunday, they might have saved him. . . .

CHAPTER TEN

IT was a chewing sound—a chewing, growling sound. Then Luke opened one eye and saw Bear eating his left sneaker, and he knew it was Saturday—and that Jo was outside his bedroom door.

"Go away!" he said.

"It's almost ten o'clock, and Mrs. Rucklehaus said to come early."

"I'm not coming."

"Why not?"

Luke wrestled with Bear, trying to figure out something to say. He didn't want to tell her that he'd squirmed and turned all night thinking of Chark— Chark lying sick on the beach while they thought he was just being lazy.

"I have to take care of the birds."

"I'll help. That way it'll go faster. I'll go ask Mom to keep Bear, and I'll meet you there in a few minutes."

Luke shoved Bear off the bed. "All right," he said finally.

"Promise? You won't just turn over and go back to sleep?"

"Promise."

He heard her running down the steps before he realized what she'd done to him. "Take the dog!" he yelled after her, but it was too late.

"THAT was a dirty trick," he said to Jo on Mrs. Bessemer's doorstep. "Take him to your mom so I can tie my shoes."

"Mom won't keep him," Jo said, grinning. She was the first one in when he unlocked the door. "Where's the sea gull. Did he come back last night after you let him out?"

"Yes." Luke glanced around, then saw the gull—one-eyed in fierce profile—staring back at him from the end of the narrow hall. "In the kitchen—on top of the refrigerator."

Not for long. The wide wings spread, then flapped. Hector glided in a straight line to the front door and landed before them—two-foot-long Hector with his strong wings barely furled.

Nine-inch Bear froze. His soft black fur stood on end, and his eyes got glassy with excitement. Completely rigid—moving as inflexibly and lightly as a toy dog jerked by a toy leash—he jumped to the left, then to the right, his quivering nose only a crunch away from Hector's powerful yellow beak.

"That's what I was afraid of." Jo grabbed the stiffened puppy and backed out the door. "We'll wait for you outside."

When the three of them were gone, Luke laughed and changed the newspapers in the cages. He was getting better at feeding Pete, or the little swallow was getting better at eating—whichever—and Joey didn't care who let him out of the aviary. Luke's one disappointment was Sally, who always nipped out and flew away as soon as he opened the little door. Didn't she remember him at all?

"Luke? It'll be suppertime before we get there."

"Coming." Might as well get it over with. He'd done it before. He could do it again.

HE could, except that this year there were an awful lot more people than last summer—so many, in fact, that they had overflowed the basement and spilled out onto the church parking lot. In the shade near the rectory, Mrs. O'Reilly and another lady were setting out pitchers of lemonade and platters of sandwiches on a table made from two sawhorses and an old door.

Luke stopped cold. "They don't need us," he said to Jo.

"Not nearly enough people, is what she said." Jo shook her head. "She probably told everyone in town that they didn't have enough people for Saturday."

"You're late!" said Mrs. Rucklehaus, with an eye as stern as Hector's. "Why ever did you bring that dog?"

"My mother won't let me leave him at home," Jo said, and added quickly, "Since you've got so many people—"

"Which do you prefer to do? Hammer or saw?"

"It doesn't matter. But since you've got so many people already—"

"I suppose you can join Mr. Tartaglino's crew," Mrs. Rucklehaus said, after studying the chart on her clipboard. "They're doing the white elephant table and the flower cart. Run along now!"

Gary Tartaglino and the older Gallagher boy were sawing planks in two lengthwise while Mr. Johnson, with his mouth full of nails and his hammer moving like a machine, fastened them together. Smooth as silk, the whole operation, Luke decided. More people would only foul it up.

Mr. Tartaglino must have thought the same thing. "Hello, Joanna. How're your folks, Luke?" He looked around doubtfully. "I'm not sure what you two can—"

"One of them can take over for me," the Gallagher boy said quickly. "I've been at it since nine and I'm hungry." He handed Luke his saw and left.

Luke knew he was stuck, so he started sawing. What he didn't know—would never have guessed—was how many people would speak to him.

"How did you say your folks were?" Mr. Tartaglino asked again.

"All right."

"Not coming, I hear. Not even for the summer?"

"No." Luke was glad Bear was yanking on his sock. He kept his head down and took his time shaking the pup off.

"That dog is a nuisance," said Mrs. Rucklehaus, who had come by with lemonade.

"Maybe we ought to take him home?" Jo offered.

"No." Mrs. Rucklehaus poured them each a glass, then gave the rest of the cups and the pitcher of lemonade to Jo. "You can do this, and I'll help here."

Mr. Johnson took the nails out of his mouth to drink. "Saw your brother out at the club," he said to

Luke. "He tells me your dad's exploring an old shipwreck this summer. That right?"

No. Paul lied through his teeth, Luke wanted to say. Instead, he nodded from behind his paper cup.

"I'll never forget when your mother had her own show at that gallery in Boston and we all went on the bus," said Mrs. Rucklehaus. "Has she had any private shows since you moved to Baltimore?"

"No." Luke reached for the saw and began working again.

"Has that puppy of Joanna Hill's had its shots?" asked Mr. Tartaglino. "I hear even cats have to get 'em."

"How about that?" said Mr. Johnson. "Rabies on the island! Bridges are a mistake. I said so at the time. With a ferry, you don't get as much riffraff."

Riffraff like rabid foxes, thought Luke. He wished that Jo would come back and get them out of here.

"Don't remember ever seeing you at the festival, Luke," said Mr. Tartaglino. "You've got to catch the tightrope act we've got lined up for this year."

"And the new dunking booth," said a familiar teasing voice.

Luke looked up at the Monsignor with a smile.

"Oh, Monsignor!" called a lady in a blue sundress. "Will we get to dunk you again this year? My boys were saying just yesterday that the dunking booth was their favorite part."

"If they come early, Mrs. Bonino. That's the only time I'll be on duty. I've got replacements for most of Saturday and Sunday."

With the Monsignor there, everyone stopped paying attention to Luke, so he settled down to work and let the talk go on around him like so much background noise. Mr. Johnson put the nails in his mouth again and began to hammer, and pretty soon the three of them were working in rhythm. All the same, Luke was glad when Jo came to say that it was five o'clock and her mother would give them a ride home.

"If that's all right?" she said to Mr. Tartaglino, letting Bear sniff at his ankle.

"Fine! Just fine!" Then he smiled at Luke. "You have grown a bit this past year, haven't you? Good hand with a saw now."

Luke felt his sunburned face grow hotter still, and he went off with Joanna.

THAT night at Mrs. Bessemer's, while he was giving Pete his cereal and apricots, the swallow chirped. His first peep, Luke thought, and smiled. Mike ought to see him now.

Then he heard the thump at the door and almost stopped breathing. Chark! He *wasn't* dead! What was he going to do? He couldn't turn Chark away from his own house, no matter what Mrs. Bessemer had said.

The thump came again, followed by what sounded like a cat's cry. Of course, it was Hector. Luke closed Pete's door.

Chark was dead, but Hector had come home. He had to put the little birds back in the aviary. Joey flew back into the big cage as soon as Luke whistled, but Sally was harder. He followed her from room to room, whistling. Finally, when Hector let out a strident cry from the other side of the door, Sally landed on Luke's shoulder and tweaked his ear—tweaked it hard enough to really hurt.

Smiling again, Luke put her gently into the cage. She was punishing him for going away. She did remember him.

CHAPTER ELEVEN

MONDAY morning Jo and Bear were waiting on the porch when Luke got back from Mrs. Bessemer's.

"You're late," Jo said cheerfully. "I told Mom to go on—that we'd walk into town if she'd give us a ride home after."

"After what?" said Luke, wary.

"After Bear gets his shot." She gave him a pained look. "Don't pretend you forgot. Yesterday you promised to go to the vet's with me."

"I didn't promise. I said I'd think about it," said Luke. It had been pretty hard to say no when he was stuffed with her mother's lasagna. Especially with Paul and the Hills sitting there listening.

"Come on," said Jo, standing up. "You can tell me about the birds as we walk. If I can ever get away from Bear I want to see Sally again."

Luke took Bear's leash. It wouldn't hurt to walk into town with her anyway.

"Hey? Can birds catch rabies?" Jo asked, as they passed the Tartaglinos' jetty.

"I don't think so," he said, but he wasn't sure. Hobo hadn't said anything about birds. "Mrs. Bessemer's sure got a lot of them. Maybe you'd better ask Doc Schaffner."

"All right, but if I'm going to do that, you have to come in with me."

"Why?" asked Luke, when they were outside the animal hospital. "You don't need me."

"Of course, I don't! Why would I—with my family—want to hang around with someone who lets me get a word in edgewise sometimes? Come on, Luke! If you keep me company, I'll ask about the birds for you."

THE front section of the hospital was half waiting room, half examining room, with a low fence between. Luke and Jo could tell from the waiting-room side that a lot of people already knew about the rabid fox.

"That schnauzer came in just ahead of us," Jo whispered in Luke's ear.

"I know that. So what?"

"We're after it! That's what. And before him," she added, as a tall man with a Doberman followed them in and took the last empty seat.

Luke was just as happy to sit on the low bench by the door, out of the thick of things. He stroked Bear. The pup was as hyper as he'd been when he met Hector, and Jo was almost as bad, keeping up a stream of whispering.

"I'm not dead sure, but I think the cocker's next— then either that old hound or whatever the lady across from us has in the carrier—then the gray kitten, the schnauzer, and us. It's not as bad as it looks because a whole family came with that gray kitten."

72

She kept her voice low, but Luke was conscious of people turning to look at them. Usually, he could stop someone from speaking to him if he didn't look at their eyes, but here there were too many eyes to miss. The longer they had to wait, the edgier he got—and so did Bear. The pup was quivering—he was one big twitch. Whenever he stepped off Luke's lap onto the bench, he left wet paw prints.

"Look, Luke! He's sweating. Poor little Bear!"

Why didn't she shut up? thought Luke. Now the man with the Doberman was watching them, too.

"What kind of a dog is that?" the man asked.

Luke let his face go blank—let the talk slide past him the way he'd done while he was sawing Saturday—and concentrated on Doc Schaffner, a calm, solid man with sandy hair. Doc gave shots to the cocker spaniel and the black-and-white hound and to the big Persian cat that the lady across from them took out of her carrier.

When the schnauzer had had his shot and gone, the mother, father, and three children all got up. The smallest child—a girl of about six or seven—put the kitten on the stainless steel table and, with the tip of her tongue sticking out of her mouth, watched while Doc Schaffner gave it an injection.

"Did it hurt Dusty?" she whispered.

"Maybe a bit. But it will keep him well."

"Does it cost?"

"No, it's free, Priscilla." Doc looked at her parents. "They'll be starting the radio announcements soon, but do what you can to spread the word. The island is paying for the vaccine. Tell everyone to bring in their dogs *and* their cats. Right away!"

73

The gray kitten left in Priscilla's arms, and it was Bear's turn. "Hold his head!" Doc said to Jo, his big, freckled hand firm on the rest of the pup.

Grim and earnest, she did it. Skillfully, Doc slid the needle in and out. "All done, Joanna," he said with a smile, handing her the trembling puppy. "You were almost as brave as Bear was."

"Thanks," said Jo, cradling the puppy close. When she started to walk out the door, Luke nudged her elbow, and she turned back. "Oh, can we ask you something? We know the fox was rabid—and we know Mrs. Bessemer's dog was found dead—"

"He was rabid, too, Joanna," Doc interrupted. "The report came back this morning." He looked at both of them closely, the way Mrs. Gray had when she asked Luke the same question. "Were either of you playing with Chark or that little fox?"

When they shook their heads, he looked relieved, and went over to wash his hands.

"But what about Mrs. Bessemer?" Jo asked. "If Chark really was rabid—" She hesitated. "I mean, is she getting the shots in time? How long does it take for a person to get rabies?"

Luke was startled. He'd never thought to ask—never questioned but that she'd gotten them in time. Had she?

Doc Schaffner smiled at Jo. "Don't worry about Mrs. Bessemer. She began the series in plenty of time. The incubation period for people is generally considered to be from two to eight weeks—but it could be as short as ten days for a bad bite on the head, or, in rare cases, as long as a year." He took some blue sheets of paper

74

from the stack on his desk and gave one to each of them and one to the man with the Doberman.

"From what I hear, Mrs. Bessemer had very little contact with the fox. Dogs transmit the virus better than wild animals anyway, so she would have been more likely to pick it up from Chark—if she picked it up at all. But with rabies, we can't take chances. Better to give the shots if there's the slightest danger because once the symptoms appear, you're a gone goose. Almost always fatal."

He sounded cheerful enough about it, thought Luke, moving toward the door. He heard Doc scrubbing off the table and lifting up the Doberman for its turn. Then he remembered.

"The birds?" he hissed in Jo's ear.

She turned. "Oh, Dr. Schaffner? Can birds get rabies?"

"Nope. Unless you count bats—which you shouldn't. Read that flier I gave you, and spread the word."

So much for that, thought Luke with relief. He folded the flier three times, put it in his back pocket, and followed Jo over to the library to meet her mother.

CHAPTER TWELVE

MRS. BESSEMER came back on Wednesday, and she was old.

For as long as Luke could remember, her hair had been gray—but now it was gray and wispy. She was wispy. Once when Hector came drooping home after a hurricane, she'd said that the starch had gone out of him. That was the way she looked to Luke now. Limp and defeated.

He tried to figure out what to do about it while he was clamming. Waist-deep in the icy water, he dragged the heavy clam rake through the mud and brought up eel grass, wads of drippy eel grass. After a bit, his luck changed and he began to get clams—enough to make a chowder for lunch one day—but still no ideas.

When he went swimming with Jo before supper, he told her how much Mrs. Bessemer had changed.

"Maybe her arm hurts her, from the shots?"

He shook his head. "I asked her and she said no. She said she was just tired—that there was nothing wrong."

Both of them knew what was wrong, but they didn't know what to do about it.

He was still puzzling over the problem while he fried the pork chops for supper. Paul had taken to buying groceries every few days. He wasn't working as many hours as he had the first week, but he was studying—and mealtimes were when they met. When he dished up the food, Luke thought about asking Paul about Mrs. Bessemer, but he wasn't sure what it was he wanted to ask.

"This is good!" Paul said, waving his fork without looking up from his pathology book.

Luke got up and held the open book over Paul's plate so that he couldn't see the table. "What is it?" he asked. "What do you think you're eating?"

"Don't be an ass! I know perfectly well what it is. Now sit down and eat your own supper." Paul tried to push the book aside without getting it into his food.

"All right," Luke said. He pretended to give in without actually moving the book. "I was afraid you were getting tired of hamburger, is all."

"Well, I'm not. You've got it cooked right tonight, too. Not dry or—" His voice trailed off. With a sheepish smile, he picked up the pork chop. "You're right, I was getting tired of hamburger. That's why I bought these." He chewed for a moment, then he said, "Do you like cooking, Luke?"

"No, but I like eating."

Paul grinned and speared another potato. "What do you do all day?"

Luke stiffened. Was Paul gearing up for another lecture about the pro shop job? "Yesterday we walked in to the library, then we went over to my old school." Luke thought of how surprised he'd been when he looked in the window. "You wouldn't believe how small the desks and chairs are!"

Paul put another forkful of potato in his mouth. His eyes glinted. "Yeah, I went back once, too. You know what, Luke? If the folks hadn't uprooted you a year ago to move to Baltimore, you'd have had a bad time this fall instead."

"What do you mean?"

"You'd have had to start riding the school bus to the mainland. Nothing after the sixth grade on the island, remember?"

Luke hadn't remembered. Maybe he'd known that island kids had to ride the bus in junior high and high school, but it had never mattered.

"I wondered why they even bothered to move," said Paul, "with that coming up next year and all, but Dad said you needed to get away more than that—and a lot sooner."

Too soon, and too much more, thought Luke. Today, the little old building where the teacher had let him learn without hassling him to speak had looked almost like a kindergarten, but he still missed it.

"Did Mrs. Bessemer come home today?" Paul asked, pushing his chair away from the table.

"Yes."

"How did she seem?"

Luke didn't know how to explain it. "Tired," he said finally.

"Maybe you'd better not go there so much. Let her rest," Paul said.

"She hasn't even been there, for heaven's sake," Luke said. "You just asked me if she'd come home.

That's why I've been taking care of the birds. Remember?"

"Oh? Right!" said Paul, sheepish again. "Well, do whatever you think. I'll wash the dishes," he added, and turned on the faucet hard.

Luke left before Paul had time to change his mind. Out on the beach, the water in the bay was a flat blue, and there were streaks of pale-colored clouds above the bridge. When he was out here, it was as if none of them had ever left the island—as if his father were still in the back room working on his book, his mother up in her studio under the eaves, looking out the dormer window every now and then at the sea, at him. His mother would know how to help Mrs. Bessemer.

SHE was out back, filling the bird feeder. Pee Wee, who was strutting around loose, let out a loud squawk and flew at Luke.

"Stop that, you spoiled feather duster!" she said, taking after the rooster with her broom. "Get in that cage! Go on! Get in there this minute." She smacked the cage closed with the flat of her broom and fastened the latch. "Time for him to go to bed anyway," she said, smiling at Luke.

He grinned. She was like her old self. Good for Pee Wee, he thought. But when they went into the house, she sat down in a kitchen chair, twisting her hands together in her lap, staring at the floor.

Luke didn't know what to do. After a bit, he heard Sally and Joey scolding, so he let them out to fly around. He fixed Pete's food and fed him. Hector came to the door and Luke let him in. Then, because it hadn't been done, he changed the newspapers in the cages and gave all the birds fresh water. Not until he had put Sally and Joey back into the aviary with the other birds, and come into the kitchen to say good-night, did Mrs. Bessemer say anything.

"Did you know he was afraid of thunderstorms?"

"I didn't know that."

She gave a little laugh. "He didn't want anyone to know. Did his best not to let on if there were people around. But no matter how far he'd wandered, he'd turn around and head home at the first hint of a rumble. Then he'd always try to sit on my lap—the big, dumb lummox."

Would she rather he left? Luke stood there, uncertain.

"He was always underfoot—always stretched out across the doorway, taking a nap. You had to watch for him every step you took or you'd break your neck." She looked up at Luke. "That's what I miss most. Having to be careful not to walk on him—knowing that if he were out, he'd come home soon. I just plain miss him being here."

All of a sudden, she laughed. "Do you know what that puts me in mind of?"

Startled, Luke shook his head.

"Nine years ago, when my Will died, people wrote a ream of nice letters about how much I must miss him, but I never told a soul about the day I missed him most."

"When was that?" Luke asked, curious.

"I think it was about three months after the funeral. I saw Mrs. Seabeck's sister from New York at Larsen's."

Mrs. Bessemer suddenly grinned at Luke. "She was over near the produce, picking out a head of lettuce—wearing orange gaucho pants and a black sequinned blouse. I remember running home from Larsen's like a bat out of hell, and Will wasn't here so we could laugh about it together."

She stood up then and walked Luke to the door. "Thanks for helping with the birds."

"Maybe I'll keep on helping, so they won't forget me," he offered. "If you want, I could stretch out in the doorway now and then, too—so you could trip over me."

It took a moment for what he said to register. The expression on her face was blank at first, and for one awful moment Luke was afraid she would take it wrong. Then the pale blue eyes brightened and she laughed.

"Where's my broom?" she demanded. "Get out of here!" she said briskly, and pretended to sweep him out the door.

WHEN he was getting undressed that night, Luke felt a stiff square of paper in the pocket of his shorts. It was the flier that Doc Schaffner had given him on Monday. Without much interest, he unfolded it and glanced at the headings. Under the last one, "How Rabies Is Spread", the word *drowsy* caught his attention, so he read that paragraph:

When an animal afflicted with the virus has the "dumb," or docile, form of the disease, it often becomes drowsy. Some household pets are un-

usually affectionate, licking and slobbering more than is customary.

He'd been right about drowsy-looking being a symptom, but none of this would have helped with Chark. That dog had been a natural-born, sleepy, slobberer long before he got rabies. Absentmindedly, Luke read on.

This slobbering is due to excess saliva caused by paralysis of the tongue and lower jaw—which makes it impossible for the rabid animal to bite or swallow. The animal is infectious only after the virus has reached the salivary glands, but the inability to bite at this stage does not render it harmless. Although biting—because it punctures the skin and permits the virus to enter the body— is the most common way for the disease to be spread, it can also be spread if the animal's saliva comes in contact with open wounds, or through the membranes of the eyes, nose, or mouth.

Open wounds . . .

Suddenly, a series of pictures passed through Luke's mind: Mike standing in Mrs. Bessemer's living room with his hand outstretched, introducing himself . . . grinning apologetically when he noticed his bleeding finger. Then Mike with his bucket and his fishing rod. . . . In his mind's eye, Luke saw the scene on the beach again—saw Chark standing on his hind legs licking Mike's face, his sunburned chest, the cut on Mike's hand.

CHAPTER THIRTEEN

LUKE woke before daylight, when it was still too early to do anything. He couldn't go to Mrs. Bessemer's to ask her what she knew about Mike, and he couldn't go talk to Jo. They didn't have much time if the incubation period was from two to eight weeks. Tomorrow—today, now—was Thursday, the eleventh day since Mike had maybe been infected with rabies. They had to find him before Sunday.

Luke threw back the covers and got out of bed. Moving quietly, he went next door to his brother's room. Paul was still sleeping, but he had promised to help last night, had understood how serious it was. Remembering that, Luke went back to bed.

Of course, he could be worrying for nothing. Maybe it would be easy to track Mike down. Maybe when he told Mrs. Bessemer what had happened, she could pick up the telephone and tell Mike to go get the shots.

BUT she couldn't.

"He brought me the baby swallow. That's all I

know about him," said Mrs. Bessemer. "I never saw the man before in my life."

"Someone had to have told him that you took care of sick birds," Jo said, her eyes gleaming. "How else would he know to bring you Pete? I mean, if he didn't know you and you didn't know him."

"He may have mentioned one of the neighbors," Mrs. Bessemer said, looking vague.

"Who?" asked Luke.

"I-I'm not sure. Perhaps it was Mrs. Seabeck."

"We'll go talk to the Seabecks then," Jo said eagerly.

After they'd been to the Seabecks', the Tartaglino cottage, and the Munsings' place, and no one seemed to know the man they were talking about, Luke got a panicky feeling that they were wasting time. "Let's go home. Paul might figure we don't need him, and go on to work."

"You go," Jo said. "I have to collect Bear before Mom kills me."

Luke took off along the side of the cottage and ran all the way to the lane. Paul was about to drive off, but waited when he saw Luke.

"What's up?"

"Mrs. Bessemer doesn't know him—doesn't know anything about him, not even his name. And neither does anyone in any of the near houses on the beach." Luke stopped for breath, his fingers white on the rolled-down car window. "What do we do now?"

Paul rubbed his eyes. "I guess you might as well go to the police station and report it so they can circulate his description."

"Can't you do it?"

Paul shook his head. "I'm late already—but I'll give you a ride. You're the one who knows what he looks like anyway."

"All right," Luke said unhappily. "Hold on. I'll get Joanna."

THE police station was down at the harbor across from the old ferry. Luke had been there three years ago to register his bike. The sick-green walls and hard benches were the same, but instead of balding Sergeant Petrillo, a young woman sat at the desk. The sign in front of her said SERGEANT LISA DUTRA.

"Good morning!" she said, smiling. "What can I do for you?"

Luke looked at Jo. She'd done the talking at the Seabecks' and the other neighbors. Why didn't she get started explaining?

Jo swallowed, then she did start. "We came be-cause—because of Mrs. Bessemer's dog, Chark. Doc Schaffner said he was rabid." She waited until the ser-geant had nodded, then she went on. "Luke and I saw Chark lick a man—and the man had a cut on his finger—and we were worried because we know the rabies virus is in the spit. I mean, licking's just as bad as getting bitten then, don't you see?"

Sergeant Dutra reached for her notebook. "I do see. What's the man's name?"

Luke leaned over to rub Bear's ears.

Jo sighed. "We don't know," she went on. "He was just walking along the beach, and when my puppy ran off and started barking at Chark, he caught him for us. Caught Bear, I mean. Then he petted Chark and Chark licked him—on the cut and everywhere."

"When did this happen?"

"Sunday—eleven days ago. And Doc Schaffner says you can get rabies fourteen days later. I mean, maybe he won't get it that soon. Maybe he didn't get infected at all. But, if he did, there's nothing anyone can do after he gets sick." She looked sideways at Luke and he nodded.

"Then we certainly need to find this man right away. Can you describe him for me? How old was he?"

Jo glanced at Luke again, but he turned away. She was doing fine. She didn't need help.

"I don't know," Jo said, sounding uncertain all at once. "Maybe he was twenty-four or twenty-five. I know he needed a shave—and he had a sunburn. A bright red sunburn." She hesitated. "I guess his hair was light and straight."

Ever so slightly, Luke shook his head. Mike's hair was dark, but none of this was as important as the stuttering. Why didn't Jo tell her that he stuttered?

"How would you describe him?"

It took Luke a moment or so to figure out that Sergeant Dutra was talking to him, then his throat sort of closed over.

"What was the most noticeable thing about the man?" the sergeant said, smiling at him encouragingly. "The first thing that comes to your mind?"

He was happy.

Luke knew he hadn't spoken the words aloud because his lips were still dry and closed. What he had to do was calm down and think through what he wanted to say so that he wouldn't freeze. He remembered a lot about Mike. He could see him clearly—the way he loped along the beach as if he were about to break into a run. . . . That grin that made you want to grin back at him. . . . Why couldn't Luke open his mouth and tell this woman these things?

"Remember, you two—this man doesn't have much time, and neither do we."

Suddenly Luke's tongue felt thick, his lips rigid. His left knee started shaking like a jackhammer, the way it had when he was up on stage in the school auditorium waiting to read those lines of poetry during assembly. He strained to speak, struggled to make a sound—any sound—to break the block, but Sergeant Dutra's face blurred. The room blurred. Luke held on to the edge of the desk and stared past Sergeant Dutra's head at the crack in the green wall.

Jo's voice came from far away, hesitant, embarrassed. "Could he write it down, do you think? What he remembers about the man, I mean?"

"Of course," said Sergeant Dutra quickly. She tore two sheets of paper off her pad and handed them to Luke and Joanna with pencils. "Each of you write down your name, address, and telephone number—then everything you can tell me about the man we need to locate."

Luke's face burned. Without looking at either of them, he sank to the floor beside Bear and used the bench for a desk. He had to forget that he'd made a fool of himself and concentrate. This was important. How would he describe Mike?

His eyes. How could he explain that Mike's eyes seemed always to be laughing? "Gray eyes," he wrote finally. "Dark, curly hair. Needed a shave. Sunburned. Wore denim cutoffs and dirty white sneakers. Medium height."

This was a waste of time. He'd just described a third of the people on the island. Nothing he had written down told Sergeant Dutra anything about Mike's gentleness with the little swallow and with Mrs. Bessemer, or the way he'd been kind to Chark. None of it gave any idea about how happy he'd been—splashing through the waves—or how he didn't seem to mind stuttering.

Dumb! After he'd been so impatient with Jo for not mentioning the stuttering, he'd forgotten it himself. "First name Mike. Stuttered when he spoke," Luke added. Then he stood up and handed the paper to the sergeant.

She read it. She read Jo's paper, too, frowning, and looked from one to the other. "What about this stuttering?" she said to Jo. "Do you remember that?"

Jo looked startled. "Oh? I guess he did stutter. I forgot."

Sergeant Dutra made a notation, then she shook her head. "We don't really have much to go on, do we? Is there anything else that either of you can tell me about this man?"

Luke thought hard. He made himself go back to when Mike had asked him about the baby swallow at Mrs. Bessemer's, then to when he was nothing but a distant figure on the beach—striding toward them with the fishing rod on his shoulder. The fishing rod? He could tell by the sudden light in Jo's eyes that she had remembered, too.

"He was a fisherman," she said. "Does that help?"

"It does indeed!" said Sergeant Dutra, laughing. "I'll get the Coast Guard on it right away. In the meantime, we can check out the bait shops and talk to the folks at Island Shellfish. Most of the regulars sell their catch to them. What kind of boat did he have?"

"Boat?" said Jo.

Not that kind of fisherman, Luke wanted to yell.

"No boat?" said the sergeant, no longer laughing.

"No boat," said Jo.

"Well, we'll see what we can do with what we've got," Sergeant Dutra said with a sigh. "I'll get some bulletins to the radio stations so they can make spot announcements, and I'll send something along to the mainland newspapers. But it's not much of a description. Could he possibly be from any of the houses along the shore?"

"We asked at the ones that were near," Jo said.

Sergeant Dutra made a note. "I'll have someone check all the houses on Shore Road. Maybe he's visiting someone. And we'll ask at the guest houses, and the hotel. If you think of anything else, please come back and tell me. As it stands now, we don't have much to go on."

"Will you let us know if you find him?" Jo asked.

"Of course!" Sergeant Dutra said. "And you two keep your eyes open. You're the only ones who know what he looks like. Don't forget that!"

CHAPTER FOURTEEN

OUT on Bay Avenue again, Jo turned on him. "What makes you think other people don't mind standing up in front of a policewoman and explaining something like that? What were you *doing* in there, Luke? It's a wonder she didn't think we were making the whole thing up, the way you acted. I know you don't like talking to people—and I've always stuck with you. I didn't even make friends with the other summer kids because of you. I've never minded being the one who asks and answers the questions, but this time you should have pushed yourself. This was different. We went in there because we *wanted* to talk to that policewoman. We weren't trying to get rid of her the way we do Mrs. Rucklehaus or Mrs. O'Reilly. You should have told her what Mike looked like without gulping and horsing around!"

Horsing around? Luke stared at her in disbelief. She didn't know what had happened to him—the feeling of disaster that had swept over him in there while he was trying to get the words out. She didn't understand that he hadn't been able to speak. Jo, who had always seemed to understand.

She stood in front of him with her chin stuck out. "What have you got to say for yourself?" she demanded.

Say for himself? That did it. That proved it. Jo hadn't a clue.

AT first he walked simply to get away from her, without caring where he walked. It was Thursday. Tomorrow afternoon the weekend tourists would glut the harbor with their cars and boat trailers. Today there were only the usual summer people wandering in and out of shops, sunbathing on the beach at the end of the street.

Luke was barely conscious of them. Now that he'd left Jo, he could think of a hundred things he ought to have said. She'd never seen him freeze up before. Until his folks had moved him to the stupid big school in Baltimore, he'd had a system. He'd stuck to people who were safe, been careful about the places he went, avoided situations where he might panic—and it had worked. People on the island knew what he was like—knew he wanted to be left alone.

All of a sudden, Luke got a whiff of mustard. How had he gotten across the road to the concession stand on the beach?

"What'll you have?" asked the guy behind the counter.

Luke began to sweat, dreading what was to come. Would he block completely the way he had at the police station? Was that what he had to worry about from now on? Not being able to speak at all?

"Sort of peaceful here midweek, isn't it?" the man said, taking off his white cap to get the breeze.

Luke nodded and swallowed. The guy looked pleasant enough.

"Live on the island, don't you?" the man said.

Without thinking about it, Luke nodded. Then he felt guilty because it wasn't true anymore.

The man put his cap back on, and both of them stood there watching the water, the people going by. Gradually the tightness went away from between Luke's shoulder blades. This was what he ought to be doing. Watching people. Looking closely at every man who was near Mike's age. They couldn't count on him wearing cutoffs and dirty sneakers all the time. After eleven days, he might not be sunburned anymore. Maybe he'd even shaved. Sergeant Dutra had said that he and Jo were the only ones who knew what Mike looked like.

"Hey? How about a hot dog?" the man behind the counter asked with a sudden smile. "The dogs are fresher than the tacos because I just grilled them."

While Luke watched in consternation, the man wrapped a napkin around a roll, the roll around a hot dog, and slathered the top edge with bright yellow mustard. "Here ya go!" he said, holding it out to Luke.

Embarrassed, Luke shook his head. "I don't think I have any—" He reached in his back pocket and felt only the rabies flier. "Money," he finished, blushing.

"Go on, take it anyway. Eat it on the beach. I've only sold a dozen so far. Maybe you'll change my luck."

Luke's hand closed around the warm bun. "Thanks!" he said with a smile, and walked on. He was glad to have the hot dog—gladder still to have said something to the man. He ought to have asked him if he'd seen a man with a fishing rod who stuttered.

Yeah, sure. Out on the beach, selling hot dogs and tacos, that guy probably saw men with fishing rods all the time. And how could you tell if someone stuttered unless he spoke to you? No point going back to ask him.

Excuses, excuses! Disgusted with himself, Luke walked out on the long, narrow wharf where rows of the bigger boats were berthed, the masts of the sailboats sticking up like toothpicks. These were the plush motor yachts and large sailboats, and here—even on Thursday—lines were being untied, motors started, sails unfurled. Here, everything was glaring sunlight and motion.

Hesitantly, Luke walked on, his Nikes going *thrump, thrump* on every plank—drawing attention to him. He tried to focus on the faces down in the boats, but it was hard because he'd trained himself not to look at people's faces. Then, all of a sudden, a man in a white motor launch caught his attention. The guy's hair was short and curly, and he was about the right height—but his back was turned. Just as Luke got close, the man leaned over and called to someone down in the cabin.

Luke could hear footsteps thudding over the planks behind him, coming his way, but he stayed where he was until the man in the motor launch stood up and turned around.

A mustache? He'd waited all this time to get a look at a man with a black handlebar mustache?

"This is a private wharf, young man. Are you looking for someone?"

Luke swung around. The man facing him had a harsh voice and eyes that were cold and measuring. Yet he had asked Luke if he were looking for someone. He'd handed it to him on a plate—made it easy for him to explain that he had to find a stranger who needed anti-rabies shots. Once Luke choked the words out, this character would turn into a helpful pussycat. So, why couldn't he do it? Why were the muscles around his mouth twitching? Why was his throat getting tight?

In angry despair, Luke turned and walked back, thrumping over the wooden planks again.

Jo was right. He hadn't done his share back at the police station. He never had. Twice, on the day it all began, Mike had gone out of his way to make friends with him—first at Mrs. Bessemer's, asking his advice about Pete, and then later, on the beach with Chark and Bear. Both times Luke had stood there like a robot because he was afraid to speak. If he'd talked to Mike, he might know where to find him now.

"Hey, Luke?"

It was Paul—standing beside the Volvo in the parking lot, waving. With an overwhelming sense of relief, Luke ran to him.

"Luke?" Paul's eyes were worried. "I ran into Joanna and she said they weren't very optimistic at the police station. They seemed to think you'd have to find him yourselves. Where do you want to look first?"

CHAPTER FIFTEEN

"I THOUGHT you had to work?"

"I did." Paul's grin was apologetic. "Then, after I worked awhile, I got to thinking you could probably use some help. I can water the greens later."

Luke felt as if a twenty-pound weight had been lifted from his shoulders. With Paul helping, they were sure to find Mike.

"No luck back there, I assume?" Paul said, jerking his head toward the wharf.

"No." Mike didn't look anything like the types that Luke had seen on the cabin cruisers in their pressed white pants and fancy yachting hats.

"Well, let's see how much ground you and I can cover in—" Paul looked at his watch. "In four hours. If I don't finish out at the club before dark, I'll have to go back in the morning." He studied the Volvo. "Might as well leave it here," he decided, and put a coin in the meter. "Do you want to split up, or shall we stay together?"

Stay together, Luke thought. "Split up," he said. "We'll cover more ground. Why don't you take the hardware store, and I'll look in the drugstore?"

"All right. have you got any money if you need it?" When Luke shook his head, Paul handed him a five. "And don't just look, Luke. Ask!"

Ask. Of course. Luke swallowed. They couldn't count on Mike being in a store when they went in to look for him. They had to describe him to the people in the stores—get them to watch for him. Luke started walking. Probably he could do that with old Mr. Thompson, if he could do it with anyone. The pharmacist just went about his business, filling prescriptions, making chocolate sodas, ringing up sales at the big, old-fashioned cash register, saying whatever needed to be said in his own dry monotone. Luke sort of admired him for it. When he told Mr. Thompson about Mike, the old man wouldn't bat an eye. But he'd watch for him.

At the door, Luke stopped dead. It was a new revolving door, all glass and brass. He backed off and looked up and down the street in bewilderment. He was in the right place. Where was the drugstore? Someone must have torn down the whole dumb building and put up a modern one with a video store on the ground floor. Video? On the island?

"Hey, Luke?" Paul called, coming up behind him.

"What happened to Thompson's?"

"Mr. Hill said the old man retired and went to live with his sister in Florida. I came back because you didn't tell me what the guy looked like."

Luke braced himself. "He was about your age, maybe a year or two older, wearing cutoffs and sneakers when we saw him. He had a bad sunburn then, too, and he needed a shave. He had dark, curly hair and gray eyes. His first name was Mike—and he stuttered."

"I sure hope he stutters when I run into him," Paul said, sounding doubtful. "Well, the new drugstore is just up the street across from the firehouse. You might as well talk to the guys in the firehouse while you're there."

"Why don't you do that?" Luke said, managing to sound cool because he'd just noticed that they were standing in front of the hardware store. "I'll ask in here."

Paul shrugged. "Six of one, half dozen of the other," he said, and started up the street.

Not really, Luke thought. At least he'd seen Mr. Lewis at the church parking lot on Saturday. Hunching his shoulders, he pushed open the screen and went in.

Right smack inside the door was a big display of roach killers, ant killers, flea killers, and fly killers—and the man at the cash register was a stranger. Sweat broke out on Luke's upper lip. Had everything on the island changed in the nine or ten months since he'd left? Where the devil was Mr. Lewis?

Luke picked up a can of roach spray and stared at it blindly, so the man wouldn't ask him what he wanted. If only he had a picture of Mike to show the guy.

A lady came into the store and began to talk to the man about paint. Luke put the roach spray down and went into the other room, stalling for time. No point even trying to speak until he was alone with the man. Would the drugstore have been easier?

Who was he trying to fool? Clenching his fists, he moved past the wall displays of toilet seats, tools, electrical fixtures. *He* was the problem—sweating, scared. He had to push himself, like Jo had said. After this came the post office, the bakery, the bank. He might as well begin. If only he had a way to begin. Then he saw exactly what he needed on the shelf of freezer supplies.

It was a long, thin box labeled COMPLETE FREEZER KIT. Luke read what it had to say on the box, just to make sure. "Everything for the home freezer: 75 square feet of heavy-duty white freezer-wrap paper in a cutting edge container, plus moisture-resistant tape and an indelible labeling pen." Yup, everything he needed.

He took out the five-dollar bill that Paul had given him, then panicked. What if Paul came back before he'd done it? Quickly, he went to the cash register and put the box and the money on the counter.

The red-faced man who wasn't Mr. Lewis rang up the sale. Luke put the receipt in the pocket with his change, but waved away the paper bag. Outside, he opened his purchase and ripped off a poster-sized rectangle of the heavy white paper. How to word it? Fast— before Paul came looking for him.

Oddly enough, it was easy. So was writing it. His printing was nice and plain, even with the thick magic marker. He grinned. It was like Mr. Elkins had said in science class. Animals who are handicapped in one area compensate so that they get pretty good in another. When he was done, he held up the big white sheet, fairly well pleased.

WANTED——FOR SHOTS

MIKE
About—25 years old
5' 10"
Gray eyes

Dark hair

Licked on cut finger by black Labrador
Sunday, June 14, on the beach
Dog was rabid!!!

Luke hesitated. For some reason, he couldn't seem to put in the part about the stuttering. Maybe he could just tell people about it. After a quick look up the street to make sure Paul wasn't in sight, he went back into the hardware store.

He held up the poster for the man to read, breathing hard, watching the man's eyes.

"Are you putting me on?" the man demanded.

"No." Luke shook his head.

"Have you reported this to the police?"

"Yes."

"Well, all right," said the man, still reluctant. "All I can say is that it better not be a hoax."

Luke shook his head again, fastening the top tapes, flattening the sheet against the glass and pressing the lower strips in place. Then he steeled himself, turning to face the man. "And, uh, he . . . he, uh . . . stutters."

The angry, incredulous look on the man's red face told Luke he'd blown it. The man thought he was some kind of wise guy. Luke wanted to shout that he was telling the truth—that the stumbling and faltering was his fault—something *he* did—that what it said on the poster was really all true. He could see that the man no longer believed him, was going to rip the poster off the window unless—

Then, through the plate-glass window, Luke saw Paul smiling at him. Pointing to the poster and smiling.

Paul came into the store. "Mr. Edgerton!" he said to the red-faced man, still smiling. "Thanks for the sign. My brother and I are anxious to get the word out as fast as we can. I take it you haven't seen anyone who answers that description?"

Right before Luke's eyes, Mr. Edgerton simmered down and started talking to Paul. No, he hadn't seen the man in question. At least, he didn't think he had. But he could certainly understand why they were so concerned.

Relieved, the complete home freezing kit under his arm, Luke went outside to wait.

CHAPTER SIXTEEN

A FEW minutes later Paul came out and sat on the steps beside him. "I dunno," he said wearily. "I went through the whole spiel both places, and they listened to me— but it's not much to go on. Where do you want to try now?"

"He was on the beach," Luke said. "Maybe we ought to check out places near the water?"

"This is an island, Luke. Everywhere is near the water."

"I know that!" said Luke, and stood up abruptly. He got a grip on himself. "How about the bank then?"

Paul looked at his wristwatch. "Good idea, but an hour after closing time." He got to his feet, too, but as if he were uneasy, tossing the car keys from one hand to the other. "Was that your idea? The wanted poster, I mean? Did you make it?"

"Yes."

"Maybe it'll help. Anyway, it gives us a lead in." He shrugged. "It's kind of awkward to march up to someone who expects you to ask for razor blades and start talking about a guy who needs shots because he got licked by a rabid dog." Paul reddened. "Anyway, if you'll make some more of those posters, we can shove them at people before we start talking—sort of get them on the right wavelength, if you know what I mean?"

Luke did. But he was surprised to find that his brother had gone through the same thought process—that even Paul sometimes felt awkward talking to people. "You want me to make some for you, too?" he asked, to make sure.

"Tell you what—let's stay together," Paul offered. "You know this guy. If someone thinks they've seen him, you'll be there to follow up. And you can make the posters. All right?"

"Sure!" said Luke. "Where to now?"

"Larsen's, I guess. Everyone has to eat."

AFTER Larsen's they went into places as they came to them, stopping at all the little gift and souvenir shops, the two gas stations, the barber shop—even the insurance building. Luke printed the signs and Paul did the talking. He was hesitant at first, but he got better at it as the afternoon wore on.

Some places there was no one to talk to. At the empty Laundromat, Luke saw a sign on the corkboard that began like his own.

<u>WANTED</u>

FOR THE SUMMER FESTIVAL
AT ST. JOHN'S
Flour & salt for clam fritters
Mayonnaise for lobster salad
Sugar for cotton candy

Mustard, relish & catsup
Also: baked goods, plants, books,
needlework & white elephants

Saturday, June 27 & Sunday, June 28
Come One—Come All

Sunday would be the fourteenth day for Mike.

"Hurry up!" said Paul. "I'll take one next door to the liquor store." He whisked the poster out of Luke's hands as he finished it. "Do one for here fast. It's getting late."

Luke tore off another piece of paper. None of the posters he had made were alike. The messages had changed gradually until it was almost as if he were writing letters to Mike.

This time he printed his name in big letters at the top of the paper.

<u>MIKE</u>
Black Labrador that licked you
on beach Sunday, June 14,
died of rabies.
You need shots!

<u>WATCH FOR THIS MAN</u>
Gray eyes, dark curly hair, approx.
25 yrs. old, 5′ 10″, 140 lbs.
May be wearing cutoffs and sneakers.
Stutters.
Needs anti-rabies shots!

Why, at last, had he been able to add the part about stuttering? How and when—between the first poster and this one—had he finally figured out that Mike wouldn't care?

"Come on!" Paul said from the doorway. "It's almost dark and we've still got to go to that cafe off the avenue and then to the hotel."

"What about the church?"

"Joanna said she'd do all three churches and the bed-and-breakfast places before she went home." Paul waited until they had crossed the street, then he asked: "Did you and Joanna have some kind of a fight? She didn't look too happy."

"I don't know," said Luke, heavy in his stomach again, remembering.

A half block away from Andy's Bar & Grill, Luke could hear the loud voices. And even before Paul opened the door, he could smell the stale beer smell.

Outside the restaurant, he spread out a square of paper on the ledge under the public telephone and made a quick poster for Paul. When his brother came out again, shaking his head, they went down Bay Avenue to the Ocean View Hotel.

There were shadowy figures on the hotel porch, rocking in a long row of rocking chairs. Luke could smell cigar smoke and citronella. In the lobby, he sat down at an unused desk, flanked by potted palms, and ripped off another sheet of paper.

"Hold on," Paul said. "Let's talk to the desk clerk first. They get a fair amount of turnover here in the summer, but he may know our man."

But the old-young man sorting papers at the main desk couldn't remember anyone who stuttered. Nor could Mr. Hargreaves, the hotel manager. About that time, Paul began to get desperate. He made the desk clerk go through the book and describe every man he could remember who had signed the register in the last three weeks. When that didn't turn up Mike, he talked the clerk into taking Luke into the kitchen to look at all the busboys. In the end, Luke made one of his biggest posters—and the two of them came out of the hotel into darkness.

"I guess I'll have to water the greens in the morning," Paul said, taking off his glasses and rubbing his eyes.

It was a hot night. Luke's head hammered and his stomach was hollow and jumpy. He'd stared at so many people, and had so many stare back at him, that he felt like one of the diagrams in his science book that showed what was inside your body—bones, organs and muscles without any skin. All he wanted to do was go home.

BOTH he and Paul swam that night after they ate, but the golden moon was gone. As he got out of the water, Luke could hear voices from the Hills' bungalow—but none of them was Jo's.

CHAPTER SEVENTEEN

THE next morning was gray—gray sea and a dull gray sky with wisps of fog.

First off, Luke went to Mrs. Bessemer's to tell her that they hadn't found Mike yet. That turned out to be a mistake because she blamed herself.

"If only I'd kept up Chark's shots. Losing him was bad, but to cause a young man like that—"

"We'll find him," Luke cut her off. If he'd brought Chark home, she'd have known he was sick—if not then, at least before he died. Then they could have looked for Mike sooner. He wadded up the used newspapers from the bird cages. "At breakfast, Paul and I heard a radio announcement telling people to watch for him, telling Mike to go to Dr. Wainwright right away—that he had the vaccine in his office. Anyway, I figure I'll go look for him on the beach again now."

He'd done it, too—walked south as far as the harbor, then all the way back to the northernmost tip of the island, the same route he'd followed a week ago when he was looking for Chark—and with no better luck. Another two hours wasted.

He saw his bowl of fresh clams when he went to

the refrigerator for orange juice. Chowder for lunch. It would give him something to do while he waited, he thought, and put a pot of water on to boil. It was getting so he didn't mind doing the cooking—especially when he could watch out the window while he chopped up things. A French tanker went past as he was cubing the potatoes, then—right at the end of the onions—a big sailboat came under the bridge.

It was tall. The mast stuck way up, and the spinnaker was a billowing blue and white. It had to be one of the twelve-meters practicing for the America's Cup races. Luke dropped the potatoes and onions into the boiling water and ran into the dining room for the binoculars.

Yup, he was right. The flag said US 21, and the boat was a beauty. Look at the way she was swerving around that little catamaran.

He caught his breath and zeroed in on the catamaran. At this distance, height and hair color were a joke, but the guy's broad shoulders and the slim build were right. Steadying the glasses, Luke brought the figure into sharper focus. The man was wearing a red-and-blue-striped T-shirt, and his skin had a sort of glow. Would Mike still be sunburned twelve days later?

It was stupid to get his hopes up. What could he actually see at this distance? Yet there was something about the guy's silhouette that made him think of Mike lifting Bear up in the air like a football. With his eyes shining, Luke ran out on the porch and across the yard to the seawall.

The catamaran moved toward the bridge. . . . Went under the bridge. Luke followed it with the glasses. Was it headed for the harbor? Or was it going around the southern point of the island? Excited, he clambered down the big rock and stumbled along the beach, trying to keep his quarry in the glasses. Looked like the guy was bypassing the harbor. Wait. No! The catamaran was turning, was heading right smack into the marina. If he hurried, he could catch up with it.

Luke climbed back up the rock and scrambled over the seawall onto the lawn. On his bike he could get to the harbor in ten minutes.

THE shore road was a solid line of traffic. When Luke turned out onto the highway from the dirt lane, he almost got picked off by a green camper. Friday, he thought, dodging in front of a Mercedes. Why did it have to be Friday? All weekend long, cars swarmed across the island like a line of ants—crawling along the shore road, then over the bridge to the mainland beyond.

The car behind him honked. Pedaling furiously, he moved over to let the Mercedes roar past, wiping the sweat off his face with his arm so that he could see where he was going. The orange Rabbit wasn't happy driving behind him either, but if he kept going over to the side, he'd never catch up with the catamaran.

At last, the bridge exit was behind him, the exhaust stink was gone, and he had the road pretty much to himself. Now, if only the catamaran didn't get lost among the other boats in the harbor. Fridays were as bad on the water as they were on the highway, and today seemed worse than usual. Because of the summer festival maybe.

Remembering the man who had hassled him about the private wharf, Luke coasted to a stop just short of it—and almost dropped his jaw.

There were catamarans all over the harbor. They had to be having some kind of special race, because every third or fourth sailing boat was split into two pontoons at the bottom. How was he going to find Mike in this mess?

Then Luke caught sight of the red-and-blue T-shirt. Letting the bike fall, he ran down to the edge of the water and waded right in. It was murky-looking but cool on his burning skin. People looked at him as if he had gone berserk, but he kept his eyes on the red-and-blue-striped T-shirt and started swimming, dog-paddling his way among the little sailboats.

"Hey, watch it, kid!"

A man in a small dory almost clobbered him with his paddle, but Luke dove under and came up sputtering alongside a big white motor yacht.

"Look at that boy!" a shrill voice screeched. "See, Dad? You can so go swimming here."

"That kid's crazy."

Luke kept his eyes on the blue and red stripes. He was almost there. Then a whistle sounded. They were probably trying to get all the catamarans in the clear, Luke decided. Must be almost time for the race. Then, suddenly, there were catamarans all around him—turning, shifting. It was like one of those funhouses at the fair where everything was done with mirrors. For a moment he almost panicked, then he grabbed the nearest double hull, dazed, trying to figure out what to do.

"Hello!" said a friendly voice. The smiling young

man in the red-and-blue-striped T-shirt offered him a hand.

Luke grabbed hold and hauled himself up, staring at him. He was about the same age as Mike, but his eyes weren't the same. Crouching on the fiberglass pontoon, Luke studied the shape of the man's face, the angles of his body. This was the guy he'd looked at with the binoculars, all right. But . . . Would he really recognize Mike when he saw him again?

Then the man spoke. "I thought you might be glad of a lift," he said, without a trace of a stutter. "Want me to drop you off as I pass the next jetty?"

Luke nodded, bushed. He'd found the man he was looking for—but it wasn't the man he was looking for.

And then he remembered that he'd forgotten to turn off the stove.

CHAPTER EIGHTEEN

THE cottage stank of burnt onions, so they ate lunch on the porch. Paul had come home too late to save the pot, but he served the clams raw, heaped on the big, fish-shaped platter that Luke liked so much.

Luke forked a pink clam out of its shell and swallowed it. "I was afraid I'd lose him. All the way to town I was afraid he'd get away."

"Good thing you tracked him down. We would have wasted a lot of time looking for the wrong man." Paul cut the bread in chunks and passed the board to Luke. "The state police are stopping all cars leaving the island, and the Coast Guard's keeping an eye out for him, too—in case he came ashore for the day from a boat. There has to be some reason no one's gotten to him."

Luke drank half his milk, buttered a chunk of bread, and helped himself to more clams. Straight out from the cottage, a black-and-white trawler chugged along slowly. Because of the man in the catamaran, Luke jammed the rest of the bread in his mouth and picked up the binoculars. The guy in the orange slicker suit had a beard longer than Mike could have grown in twelve days, but Luke kept watching while the man reeled in the net, rolling it on the big spool—shaking the fish into the hold as he wound. When the spool was full and fat, the boat turned around and chugged back the direction it had come, unrolling the net with its bright orange floats into the water again.

"That guy look familiar?"

"No." Luke lowered the binoculars.

"Want to go back to town? Try the bank maybe?"

Luke shook his head. The town was papered with posters. His scraped his clamshells onto the fish platter, then studied the tiny cut he'd gotten on his hand. "There's one thing we could do," he said abruptly. "Sergeant Dutra figured Mike wasn't a regular fisherman because he didn't have a boat. At least, we didn't see a boat. But Mike said the cut on his hand came from tangling with a lobster." He watched Paul's face. "I know the Coast Guard checked at the fishing wharf, but—"

"But we could check, too," Paul said, smiling at him.

"Come on, then!"

"Aren't you forgetting something?"

Luke flushed. "Oh, sure." He picked up the platter and their glasses.

Paul took them from him. "That's not what I meant. You go get your marking pen and that roll of paper."

"Oh? Sure!" Luke said again, but with a smile.

A few minutes later, sliding into his side of the Volvo, he realized he felt different today—more as if he and Paul were partners.

AT the old ferry, Paul stopped the car but kept the motor running. "Where specifically?"

"Keep on past the yacht basin, then take the next left." As they got closer, Luke added, "Dad parks over by Island Shellfish and walks back. Jo said her brother Alex drives right out on the wharf and waits for a lobster boat to come in."

Paul drove past the yacht mooring where Luke had looked yesterday and stopped at a longer, wider wharf with sheds on it and gas pumps way out at the end. He shook his head when he saw the amount of traffic—cars and pedestrians—moving back and forth on the dock. "Alex can drive out there, if he likes. I'm going to let you walk it. Just leave me a poster."

Luke nodded, and got out into a cloud of squabbling gulls.

"I'll go ask around at Island Shellfish," Paul said. "They buy and sell a lot of lobster, and they've got a parking lot."

"All right," said Luke. He picked his way among the fish heads and entrails that the gulls had dropped, dodged the birds when they swooped down to retrieve them, and went stumbling over the thick coils of rope that seemed to be everywhere. When he got about half-way out, the planks began to get farther apart, and he could see the water underneath.

"Watch out!" came a shout, and a big man pushed past him with a dolly full of crates. After the dolly came a pickup truck, and behind the truck, a green Volkswagen.

Way too much traffic in the middle, Luke decided, and headed for the side. The tide was coming in, and all the moored fishing boats thudded against their rubber-tire bumpers, shaking the dock. Finally, in a boat tied up just ahead, he saw some men in boots and gloves tossing live lobsters into big water tanks in a shed.

For a moment Luke felt the same excitement he'd had that morning chasing after the man in the catamaran, but this time he held back. No more going off half-cocked. What he had to do was look at the lobstermen one at a time, slowly and calmly. Breathing hard, he focused on the man who was closest—the one with the cigar—then his ears got a message through to his brain.

He didn't understand what the two lobstermen were saying. He didn't understand because they were speaking Portuguese. Of course. He should have re-membered that more than half the fishermen and lob-stermen on the island were Portuguese.

After that he listened as he walked. When he found an English-speaking crew, he held out his poster hesitantly.

"Cutoffs?" said one burly guy, laughing. "You mean short pants?" He laughed even louder, pointing to his sodden work jeans, mockingly slicing at both thighs with the edges of his hands. "Cutoffs!" he hooted.

Of course, thought Luke. Cutoffs would be stupid. The heavy pants the lobstermen wore protected them the same way gloves did. And when they weren't work-ing, they still wouldn't wear cutoffs. It didn't fit. Didn't fit any more than a sunburn would.

He walked on, looking at and listening to other men on other lobster boats. He stopped to watch a small boat tie up long enough for its two-man crew to shovel a load of silvery fish into a barrel and carry it into a long shed. When that boat pulled away from the dock, Luke walked back to look for Paul, who was waiting for him at the curb.

Luke could tell he hadn't had any luck either. "We're wasting our time," he said quickly. "He couldn't have been a lobsterman. He's not any kind of fisherman who fishes for a living."

Paul waited until he was back in the car. "We can't be sure yet."

"Yes, we can. We came here to look for him because he had a cut on his hand. These guys wear gloves most of the time, but their hands are pretty tough anyway. And Mike's sunburn was new—raw, even— and their skin is like shoe leather. And the way he talked—"

"What do you mean?"

"It's not just that he wasn't Portuguese." Luke shook his head hard. "I listened to some others, too— and even when Mike stuttered, he spoke plainer than they did. Different."

"Not an island accent?" Paul didn't sound convinced. "Come on! You and I were raised here, and we don't have one. I don't believe there is an island accent, as such."

"I don't think he's an islander, but that's not what I'm talking about," Luke said, impatient. "He sounded more—more—"

"Educated?" Paul offered, putting the key in the ignition.

"More educated than the fishermen," said Luke. "But besides that, he talked as if he were used to making himself understood—like Mr. Leonard."

"Who's Mr. Leonard?"

"He's the assistant principal at the school I went to last year."

Paul raised his eyebrows. "Hauled you into the office, did he?"

Luke grinned. "He said I was a change of pace. He said most of the complaints he got were about kids who never *stopped* talking."

"All right. Mike's not a lobsterman," Paul said, tracing the steering wheel lightly with his forefinger. "Where does that leave us?"

"Like I said, I don't think he's even an islander."

"For the same reasons?"

"That and others." Luke thought for a moment. "If he lived here, someone would have recognized him from the bulletins and posters. And if he'd lived here a year ago, Jo and I would have seen him on the beach. You could tell he liked the water.

"In fact, he liked it so much, I doubt if he'd been around it much." Luke brightened because maybe that would help. "I'll bet he was just here for that weekend— maybe just for the day?"

"Great!" Paul said tiredly, leaning back in the car seat. "So he's gone home to the Bronx. How do we find him?"

"I don't know," Luke said. What hadn't they done that they could still do? It was almost five o'clock. If Mike wasn't on the island, how could they get word to him in time? Luke tried to imagine Mike standing outside the Convention Hall in Baltimore, but he didn't fit. That was because of the cutoffs and sneakers. How was he dressed now? How did he feel?

How *did* he feel? Maybe that was an angle. If Mike had been infected with the rabies virus, how would he feel twelve days after that had happened? Did people get sick all of a sudden, or did it happen gradually? The flier said that the vaccine wouldn't help after the symptoms showed up, but suppose there were early warning signs? Some kind of clue before the virus took over? A rash, maybe?

"What's the first thing that happens when you get rabies?" he asked Paul.

"At the end it's convulsions and paralysis, but I don't know how it starts. Why?"

"If we knew what he was going through now, we could still warn him, don't you see? If it was something—something unusual, I mean." He twisted around to face Paul. "Look! Suppose—just suppose—that before a person actually got sick from rabies, he turned blue in the face?" He shook his head when Paul tried to interrupt. "I know that's dumb. I'm just using it as an example. But suppose it was true—and we got the radio stations to make announcements about it. Then suppose there was a man with a blue face in a hospital somewhere, and he didn't know what was wrong with him and the doctors didn't know what was wrong with him, and—"

"Enough with the blue faces already!" Paul said, rolling his eyes in mock despair. He grinned at Luke and started the car. "I see what you're getting at, though. Let's go talk to Dr. Wainwright."

CHAPTER NINETEEN

EVEN though Paul didn't say a word about blue faces, Dr. Wainwright seemed to think they were crazy.

"What you're suggesting is preposterous," he said in his flat, dry voice. "Even irresponsible. If you were to broadcast a warning such as you suggest, every idiot with a headache from too much sun would start frothing at the mouth."

"Is a headache the first symptom?" Paul asked.

"One of them," said the doctor. "Also, irritability, loss of appetite, restlessness, anxiety, and depression." He stood up and took off his white coat. "I spent the last fifteen minutes explaining all this to a reporter from the *Island Weekly* who wanted to write a panic article. Urging people to have their pets vaccinated is a good idea, but highlighting a list of common symptoms in the media—locally or nationally—would be foolish."

Dr. Wainwright looked at Luke. "Did you witness this, er, licking incident?"

Luke nodded.

"He's been looking for the man," Paul said quickly. "Luke and Joanna Hill are the two people who saw it happen and would recognize him."

Dr. Wainwright slid his arms into his seersucker jacket and picked up his bag. "Presumably, he would recognize you as well?"

"Yes," said Luke, on guard.

Dr. Wainwright took out his keys and motioned them toward the door. "I have to lock up here and go to the hospital. Why don't you go over to the veterinarian's office, young man? That's where I sent the reporter—and the photographer he had with him. Tell them that you know the man who was infected with rabies—and vice versa. Don't let that jackass make a soap opera out of it," he admonished Paul with a tight grin. "Just see that they feature the boy's picture with an appropriate caption. It might help, you know."

"It can't hurt," Paul agreed, and the three of them left the building.

Dr. Wainwright got into the old Cadillac parked at the curb and drove off, and Luke started up the street.

"Where are you going?" Paul called after him.

Luke's face got red. Did Paul think he was trying to duck out of this deal with the reporter? "To get Jo," he said. "I'll meet you there in five minutes."

HE knew she'd promised to help her mother sort secondhand books in the church basement, and that was where he found her—where he told her what Dr. Wainwright wanted them to do.

"Talk to a newspaper reporter?" she repeated after him slowly.

Her eyes measured him, and he waited warily. She would come because she wouldn't let Mike down. That didn't worry him. Now, even her yelling at him on

Thursday didn't worry him. But things were different between them. He wanted her to say it so he could be sure it was still all right.

"Will you come?" he asked.

"Why not?" she said, and looked him right in the eye. "Mike's more likely to recognize you with all three of us in the picture."

EXCEPT for Doc Schaffner, the newspaper people were the only ones in the animal hospital. The reporter's name was Tony DeCarlo, and the photographer was a tall, red-haired woman in overalls who said her name was Megan.

"Are you saying that you actually saw this fellow get bitten by a rabid dog?" Tony asked, cutting off Jo who was trying to explain. "You were right there? Where did the dog bite him?" He waved his pencil at Megan. "Get a close-up of these kids with their puppy."

"He didn't get bitten," Jo said.

"Move in closer," said Megan. She took Luke by the shoulder and jammed him against Jo, almost knocking their heads together. "What a cute puppy! He looks exactly like a little black fox!" she said, picking up Bear. "Don't you dare bite me, you little devil. Here! Hold the little beast so I can get him in the picture."

Luke took Bear and went back to staring at Doc, who was bandaging a cat's leg. Usually when someone battered him with words, he could shut them out, but these two were too close and too loud. The fact that DeCarlo kept writing things down in his little notebook didn't help either.

"Dr. Schaffner says it makes a difference where—on the body—a victim gets bitten," DeCarlo said, without looking up from his notes. "Now, where did you say this man—"

"Hold it!" said Megan.

A flashbulb went off. Luke shut his eyes, and Bear jerked.

"That'll be a great shot," said Megan, head bent over her camera. "Now, let's try one of the young lady holding the puppy and you"—she poked Luke with her finger—"you looking worried as if the little fellow had just been bitten by a mad dog."

"Nobody got bitten!" Jo almost yelled. "The man we saw was licked on a cut on his finger."

"Licked? You mean he wasn't even hurt?"

"He'll die if we don't find him," said Jo. "How hurt can you get?"

Doc broke in. "It's like I told you, DeCarlo. The virus is in the saliva of the infected animal, and the man in question was licked on an open wound."

"Licked won't get any attention. And attention is what you want, isn't it?" DeCarlo shook his head, uneasy. "Why don't we just say he got bitten?"

"Because then he won't realize that he's the man we're looking for," Luke said, without thinking about it. DeCarlo had missed the point. "Dr. Wainwright said that if you put a picture of us in the paper, Mike might recognize us and come in to get the shots."

"Why not?" said Megan, as the light flashed again. "A blow-up of my best shot on page one with a caption that says: HAVE YOU SEEN THESE CHILDREN? How does that sound?"

"As if we'd been kidnapped," Jo said.

"Never mind. We'll think of something. Stand still, kids. I want to take a couple more to be safe."

"Wait a minute," Tony DeCarlo said. "Why does it matter where someone gets bitten, Doc?"

Doc Schaffner put the bandaged cat back into its cage. "The farther the bite is from the brain, the better," he said. "Bites on the head, neck, shoulders, or hands means that the virus reaches the brain sooner than a bite on the lower part of the body. What you have to remember is that the virus travels along the nervous system—not the bloodstream."

"Hold the puppy higher," Megan said. "And point its nose to the side. You have to take a picture of a black dog in profile unless you want it to look like a blob."

Head, neck, shoulders, hands . . . Luke turned Bear's muzzle toward Jo, hearing the words over again as if Doc were still saying them. Did he mean that a bite on the hand was as bad as one on the head? No, he meant what he had said, that it was worse than a bite lower down—say, on the leg or foot.

The flashbulb went off again and then Megan began to put the camera away. "That ought to do it, kids. Let me have your names and addresses."

"I'll give you those," Paul said from the doorway. He took the papers Megan gave him and filled them out. "Now, where and when will the photograph appear?"

"Front page. *Island Weekly*. Next Wednesday," said Tony DeCarlo.

"Next Wednesday?" Luke said, unbelieving.

"Next Wednesday?" Paul and Jo repeated in unison.

122

"Hey, look, folks! We're a weekly. Wednesday's the day we come out!"

Great! thought Luke, and headed for the door. There went their last chance.

CHAPTER TWENTY

NO one talked much on the way home.

Paul had to go to work after he dropped them off, but Luke couldn't think of anyplace else to look anyway. Jo's mother invited him to supper, but for once in his life he wasn't hungry. Maybe because all they talked about at the Hills was not finding Mike.

"Well, heaven knows you looked hard enough for him," Mrs. Hill said, as she got up to clear the table. "And everywhere I go, I see your posters. I really don't know what else you could have done."

"We could have *found* him," Luke said, then he closed his mouth.

He was startled—and so were Mr. and Mrs. Hill. It was the first whole sentence he'd spoken to them in his life.

"Want me to stop by for you in the morning?" Jo asked at the door.

"Sure!" said Luke airily. He crossed both their lawns and went up on his own porch. After all these years of avoiding it like the plague, he was going to the summer festival with Jo—but it would probably be a waste of time. Mrs. Hill had praised them for looking for Mike, but that wasn't any use. It was like studying for a test. You could brag about the hours you spent rereading the textbook, but what mattered—the only thing that mattered—was how well you did on the exam. And he'd flunked.

He'd done a lot of different things in the two weeks he'd been back on the island, but none of it had done Mike any good. Mike still didn't know what was going to hit him.

Luke stared out at the bay. One small sailboat hurried home in the dwindling light. The sky and the water were getting close to being the same color, darkening, changing, becoming a more intense blue.

He thought about going over to Mrs. Bessemer's, but decided not to. Restless, he went inside.

The chicken and mashed potatoes that he'd eaten at the Hills had filled him up, but he went to the kitchen from habit. He washed up the few dishes in the sink because he had nothing better to do. Carefully, he dried the heavy fish-shaped platter, polishing its bright blue tail.

When he was little, he had liked to trace the shape of the fish with his forefinger, the way he liked tracing the raised stag on the brown iced-tea pitcher in the kitchen in Baltimore. Once he'd asked his mother why she hadn't brought the platter with them. She'd said it belonged on the island. At the time, Luke had been comforted to know that she'd thought it all through. What should stay and what should go. The fish platter had stayed. Luke and the pitcher had gone.

Uneasy, he moved on through the cottage. In his father's study, he saw the faceless photographs of undersea divers on the wall and knew that they were all pictures of his father.

Upstairs, looking out the window of his mother's studio, he saw how dumb he had been to believe that his parents would move back to the island. He could almost feel their new lives holding them. But no matter that moving away had turned out to be good for them—Mom meeting other artists, Dad getting a chance at the Cyprus shipwreck—he guessed maybe they *had* left the island for his sake—at least partly. And maybe they'd been right to do it.

Even though he wasn't sleepy, Luke stretched out on his bed and watched the bridge lights blink, trying not to think about Mike anymore.

They weren't going to find him in time. In books things came out right at the end, but this was real. Angrily, Luke slammed his pillow over on the cool side. There was a mouse on one of the overhead beams. He couldn't see it but he could hear it running around.

That's what they'd been doing—he and Jo and Paul. Running around in the dark. The worst of it was, this thing was only happening to Mike because he'd stopped to help them. He needn't have stopped. Luke could have caught Bear. If Chark had licked him, he would have known to get the shots. He would have been right here.

Next door, Bear began to bark. Luke sat up and listened as Paul drove the Volvo into its parking place at the back of the yard. But when he heard Paul's footsteps on the stairs, he rolled over on his stomach, rubbed his eyes hard on the pillow, and pretended to be asleep.

After a bit, his bedroom door opened very quietly. Luke breathed in and out, in and out, without moving.

Pretty soon he heard water running in the bathroom, and he knew that Paul had gone.

Outside, the wind shifted. He could smell the unmistakable rank odor of a skunk somewhere close. Checking out garbage cans most likely, but Paul had put a big rock on top of theirs.

What didn't make sense was that if Mike were still on the island, they ought to have tracked him down. Even though Luke had been wrong about him being a lobsterman, even though the stupid newspaper didn't come out until next Wednesday. The radio announcements were still being made every few hours; the state police were stopping outgoing cars at both bridges; the Coast Guard was checking boats. To miss all that Mike had to have left after the first Sunday—the day Chark had licked him—and before the second Wednesday, ten days later, when Luke had read the flier about rabies. And, if he had, he didn't have a chance.

Luke groaned. The sheet under him was hot as fire, but after a while he broke into a sweat. Toward morning he fell asleep and dreamed that he was dying of thirst— writhing on the floor in agony from thirst. He dreamed that Paul brought him a tall drink of ice water, but he couldn't swallow.

CHAPTER TWENTY-ONE

LUKE knew he couldn't not go to the festival, but he woke with a sick dread that was like a rock in his stomach. It stayed with him while he dressed, and seemed to grow heavier still as he and Jo walked to town with Bear.

"This won't do any good," he said.

Jo shrugged. "Mom said Sergeant Dutra arranged for someone to make announcements over the loudspeaker every two hours, but that won't do any good either if it's the same sound system as last year."

"Or if he only stays an hour and a half," Luke wisecracked. But nothing was funny. Mike was almost certainly miles away. If he weren't—if, against odds of ten thousand to one, he did turn up at the festival, he and Jo might not spot him. Of course, he might recognize them if they had Bear. If the puppy lasted that long.

It was ten degrees hotter than it had been all week— so sweltering that Luke could see wavy layers of hot air hanging over the pavement. By the time they got to the field where the festival was, Bear was panting hard and kind of quickstepping, trying to keep his feet off the hot sidewalk.

"Let's get in out of the sun," Jo said, motioning toward the long orange tent. She ducked inside and Luke followed her. "Mom brought a Thermos of ice water. I've got to find her and give Bear a drink. You go around that way. If you see the bookstall before I do, come meet me with the Thermos."

Luke started walking the direction she'd pointed, still blinking from the glare. It wasn't as crowded in the tent as he'd thought it would be, but it was bad. Sounds came at him from all sides, hard and fast like baseballs. On the other side of the canvas, Gary Tartaglino was auctioneering through his nose in a loud voice, and, inside, the man at the roulette wheel was ballyhooing his prizes. Luke didn't see Jo's mother anywhere, but the next table had food—coffee cake with a crumbly top and plates of triangular doughnuts.

Doughnuts . . . It seemed as if he'd been hungry ever since they got to the island. This morning, instead of breakfast, Paul had left a stack of quarters on the kitchen table. Luke's hand went to his pants' pocket and found two of them. He pointed at the pile of crusty doughnuts, his eyebrows raised in question.

"A quarter apiece," said the woman behind the table, taking the coins from his hand. She had a portable fan going full blast and an angry red sunburn on her face and neck, right down to the V-shaped opening of her blouse. "I did the auctioneering for the first half. Burnt myself to a crisp," she said, handing him two doughnuts in a paper napkin.

Embarrassed, Luke moved on, walking faster. There were more babies here than he'd ever seen in one place—babies around people's necks, in slings, babies sprawled out in strollers. Suddenly he realized that Gary Tartaglino's bellowing had stopped. The auction was over, and the tent was filling up with sweating, red-faced men and women, glassy-eyed from the sun. He shoved the last bite of doughnut into his mouth and moved on past a table of costumed dolls, past the handiwork booth, and found the secondhand book table.

Jo was already there, and her mother was pouring ice water from the Thermos onto a towel. She emptied a box of books on top of those on her table, folded the wet towel in the bottom of the carton, and put Bear on it.

"Mom says Bear's having a sort of heat stroke," Jo said. She'd gone pale beneath her freckles, so Luke knew she was scared. "She's going to aim her fan at him. She says he'll be all right if we keep him quiet for a while."

"Bear will be fine!" Mrs. Hill said firmly. "I'll give him more water after a bit. You two go get something to eat and leave him to me."

Luke followed Jo toward the exit, the doughnuts sitting heavy on his stomach. They stepped out into blinding sunlight, and for a moment he was stunned by the brightness and the noise. About fifty feet from the tent he saw the rough wooden bandstand that Mr. Lewis and his two sons had built for the Monsignor. Different groups were scheduled to play both afternoons, but now the bandstand was empty except for some stereo equipment with loud rock blaring out of its speakers.

"That's where they'll make the announcements

from," Jo said, talking into Luke's ear so that he could hear her. "Mom thinks they made the first one about twenty minutes ago, but she wasn't sure what they were saying."

Luke could believe it. It was worse out here than it had been in the tent. Everything too noisy, too bright. All the food stands had awnings of fluorescent blue plastic, and the air smelled of mustard and deep-fry fat.

"I want a doughboy," said Jo.

Luke began elbowing his way through the crowd. The first booth they came to served clam fritters, and the second one—with a big ice chest—had lobster salad sandwiches and cold watermelon. Eyes half-closed against the sun, they moved on to a third stand and saw the big, sugary puffs draining on a row of spread-out paper towels.

Luke held up two fingers and a handful of quarters, but the man behind the counter shook his head.

"You have to buy tickets," he said. "We can't take cash."

"Where?" asked Jo.

"In the tent—across from the roulette wheel."

"I'll wait for you here," Jo said, stopping to watch some little kids toss darts at a board full of balloons.

Luke pushed his way back into the tent. A lot of people wanted to buy tickets, so he got in line and waited until it was his turn.

"How many?" asked the dark-haired young man, smiling.

Luke opened his mouth, then closed it again and stared at the man in astonishment.

CHAPTER TWENTY-TWO

"IS anything the matter?" the ticket seller asked.

Luke shook his head, sick with disappointment. The guy was only another dark-haired young man. His eyes were smaller than Mike's and his chin was wrong.

"Do you want tickets, or not?"

Luke spilled out quarters without looking up.

The man counted them and gave him a strip of tickets. "Move along now, kid," he said uneasily.

The people in the line behind Luke stepped aside to let him by. All of a sudden he wished he had never come back to the island. Never met Mike.

But the fox would have come anyway, part of him argued. The fox would still have given Chark rabies. And Jo and Bear—and Mike—would still have walked along the beach. Probably Chark would have licked Mike even if Luke had gone to Greece.

But then he would never have known about it. Why did he have to know? Now he would always be looking for Mike—even when it was too late. He would always wonder what had happened to him.

"What's the matter, Luke?" Jo asked worriedly. "Is Bear worse?"

"I thought I'd found Mike, but I was wrong," he said. He watched the light come and go in her eyes in the time it took him to say it. "He wasn't the right man at all. He didn't sound like him, and he didn't really look like him."

"What do we do now?" she asked.

"Keep looking," he said, angry with himself for wasting time. "Keep moving around. Want a Pepsi with your doughboy?"

"Why not?"

Now there were lines at all the refreshment stands. Luke got the Pepsis while Jo waited for the doughboys, then they walked side by side, looking at faces in the crowd. The man at the penny pitch was too old, and the magician was a wispy man with a pasted-on mustache.

He and Jo moved on to the dunking booth. They got there just as the Monsignor was climbing out of the water for the last time that day.

"Ladies and gentlemen," he began, his old black suit sopping wet and his clerical collar askew. "Ladies and gentlemen, I warned you that I was working only part-time in the dunking booth this summer festival. Now, let me introduce my replacement for today—Father Sullivan, newly ordained and fresh up from Connecticut this very hour."

The Monsignor took off his wet collar and undid the top button of his black shirt. Luke edged in closer to get a look at the dunking booth. The plank was high above the water and protected by rope netting so that the balls could be aimed at a target lever—and not at the person sitting on the plank.

"I very much regret not being able to persuade Father Sullivan to dress properly for the occasion," the Monsignor finished with a grin, "but he only drove up for a few hours, so he didn't bring his blacks with him. Just remember—he's a priest all the same. Go for him—all you altar boys out there!"

The crowd roared with laughter as a sober-faced young man in swim trunks and a green T-shirt scrambled up the ladder at the side of the tank and settled himself on the plank with a shy wave. Luke stared hard at him and his stomach lurched. He looked over his shoulder, but Jo was nowhere in sight.

This was stupid. It was happening to him again—the way it had with the ticket seller and the man on the catamaran. The three men were nothing alike. He was imagining things—that was his problem. Joanna would sort it out for him. Where was Jo?

In front of him and behind him a line began to form, and he was in it—about four people from the front. Luke craned his neck to look around the man ahead. The guy smelled of beer and he was eating clam fritters out of a greasy bag.

"Doesn't look old enough to be a priest, does he?" the man said, tilting his beer bottle for another swallow.

Luke stepped out of line to get a better look. Until today, he'd figured he would know Mike when he saw him, but now he wasn't certain. This Father Sullivan had to be older than Paul, but his cheeks were smooth and pink, his hair as soft as a little boy's. He didn't seem as sure of himself as Mike had—but there was something about him all the same. Where was Jo?

"Hey, *bang-o!* The kid got him!" yelled the man in

front of Luke, crushing the empty fritter bag into a wad. "Did you see that? That high school kid dunked him."

Father Sullivan came up out of the water like Superman bursting out of a telephone booth, shaking the wet hair out of his face. Once he'd climbed the inner ladder and plonked himself on the plank again, he looked a lot more relaxed. The next person in line was a girl about seven or eight years old. Father Sullivan gave her a big smile and pretended to be afraid that she would knock him off the plank, too.

Luke stared hard at him. Now that it was wet, the priest's hair was darker and curled up some. And on the middle finger of his right hand—the hand he was using to squeeze the water out of his hair—there was a tired-looking Band-Aid.

CHAPTER TWENTY-THREE

IF he were Mike, the Band-Aid could be covering the cut he got from the lobster. But why hadn't it healed before now? What about the sunburn? Was his skin peeling under the T-shirt?

The little girl threw wide, then tossed her second and third balls without stopping to take aim. Father Sullivan shook his head at her and grinned.

"Hey, lady?" the clam fritter man said to the woman ahead of him. "All of us waited in line to buy tickets. If you want to dunk the priest, you go buy tickets, too." He turned to Luke, aggrieved. "The nerve of her, trying to make them take cash when—" He broke off as the woman gave him a dirty look and left, then moved up quickly to take his turn.

Luke stood there, uncertain. If Father Sullivan *was* Mike, someone had to tell him about Chark right away so that he could go get the shots. Did Dr. Wainwright have office hours on Saturday? Was he standing by in case Mike was found, or would they have to go look for him? Luke glanced over his shoulder, but he couldn't see past all the people bunched up around the dunking booth. Jo probably figured he had this spot covered.

136

Luke turned as the man ahead of him missed with his second ball. When it ricocheted off the tank and almost hit Luke in the face, Father Sullivan grinned at him sympathetically. Great! But why didn't he say something? Luke thought. If only he could hear the priest's voice—hear if he stuttered.

"I'll get you this time, Father!"

Father Sullivan gave the guy an easy smile and kind of rocked on the plank as if he were teasing him. He sure didn't look sick, Luke thought. Maybe he was making a mistake. If this guy was Mike, why hadn't he seen the posters? Heard the radio announcements? Then Luke remembered what the Monsignor had said about the young priest having driven up from Connecticut. That fit. If he'd been here a couple of weeks ago—and then gone back to Connecticut—

The clam fritter man missed with his third ball and swung around on Luke angrily. "Hey, you? Sell me three tickets quick, will you?"

Luke held out his strip of tickets. The man helped himself, looking sheepish, and pressed some money into his hand. The guy owed him a favor now, Luke thought. Maybe he could get him to talk to Father Sullivan. But how? The guy would think he was joking. Luke could never explain it to him. Why hadn't he brought the poster paper? He didn't even have a pencil. Whoever explained about Chark was going to have to yell. The rock music was still blasting out at eighty or ninety decibels, and the big, rectangular dunking tank was roped off so that you couldn't get close. Even the smallest kids had to stand back ten feet to throw.

The clam fritter man made another bad pitch and

groaned. So did Luke—softly. Pretty soon he'd be up.

The big guy wound up and threw again. This time he connected. The ball hit the target, the target triggered the lever, and the right side of the plank dropped—sliding Father Sullivan into the water again.

"*Yeeee-owww!*" the clam fritter man screamed in delight.

Luke looked around wildly for Jo—for Sergeant Dutra—even for the goofy reporter, Tony DeCarlo. Where was the Monsignor? He had to be here someplace and he knew Father Sullivan. He could tell him to get the shots.

But why hadn't he already told him? Why hadn't he realized that Father Sullivan was the man they were looking for?

Luke swallowed. Was he wrong after all? If only he could remember exactly what Mike looked like. How much difference did it make when someone hadn't shaved for a couple of days? Paul looked pretty much the same, but he didn't get much stubble.

"Whoopee!" the clam fritter man yelled, waving at the young priest as he climbed back on the plank, dripping. "Your turn now, kid," he said, pushing Luke forward.

Gary Tartaglino's middle boy was taking tickets. He tore three from the strip in Luke's hand and gave him three balls. Breathing unevenly, Luke stepped up to the rope, staring at Father Sullivan. Was he imagining this or not? The Monsignor had been in on the search from the beginning. He knew that the man Chark licked had a stutter. If this were Mike, surely the Monsignor would have figured it out.

Then Father Sullivan winked at him. Winked at him and grinned just the way Mike had when Joanna thanked him for helping Bear—when both Luke and Mike knew that Bear hadn't needed any help.

It was Mike. Luke knew it. Now he had to tell him to go find Dr. Wainwright—that Dr. Wainwright had the vaccine. His tongue felt swollen but he tried to clear his throat.

"Throw the ball!" someone behind him shouted. "Go on! Pitch!"

Luke's right hand fingered the ball, curved around it automatically as if he were playing softball with his father. He let his right arm wind up for the pitch and then he caught himself, remembering what he was here for.

Father Sullivan bounced up and down on the plank, kind of egging him on. Luke stared right back at him, meeting his laughing eyes, rehearsing the words in his mind: Remember the black Labrador that was so friendly on the beach? The big black dog that licked your cut hand?

"Throw the ball!" a kid yelled. "Take your turn!" another voice shouted.

The young priest smiled, and Luke began to sweat. It should have been so easy to tell him. This wasn't something he had a choice about. He *had* to tell him.

"Come on, kid! Throw!"

Dripping with perspiration, Luke dropped the balls back into the bucket and ran. He had to find Joanna. Jo would tell him.

CHAPTER TWENTY-FOUR

SHE was over at the pony rides, leading a tubby gray pony by the halter. Tommy Seabeck, who lived up the beach, walked alongside, steadying a little girl in the saddle.

"I found him," Luke said to Joanna. "Come on!"

Jo's eyes shone. She handed the halter to Tommy and ran to catch up with Luke, who was already headed back. "Where is he? Where did you find him?"

"At the dunking booth. Hurry up."

"Where at the dunking booth? Taking tickets?"

"In it. Getting dunked."

"I don't understand. When I left, the Monsignor was introducing that Father Sullivan—"

"That's him. He's Mike. The Monsignor said that he just came from Connecticut today. So he couldn't have heard the radio announcements. He probably doesn't even know there's been rabies on the island."

"Didn't you tell him?"

He was getting *her* to tell him. Couldn't she understand that much?

"Luke?"

They were back at the dunking booth, only now Luke had lost his front position. They were on the outside of a close-packed crowd.

"Are you telling me he doesn't know yet?" Jo demanded.

"Yes," said Luke, ashamed. But there wasn't time to be ashamed. "You tell him. We'll have to push in closer. Maybe we ought to go around back?"

Jo's expression was doubtful. "I don't understand. I told the Monsignor about the man we were looking for." She followed Luke as he squirmed through the crowd.

"Look!" he said, when they were close enough for her to see for herself. "Don't you recognize him?"

Jo studied the smiling young man on the plank. "Yes," she said finally. "I recognize him. He said five o'clock mass on Saturday two weeks ago."

A burst balloon—that was what he felt like. Disappointed wasn't a big enough word. Then he realized that what she had said didn't matter. "So what? He's Mike just the same. He just looks different because he's shaved and cleaned up. Look at him again."

He could see why it was hard for her. Mike was propped up on one elbow now, laughing at a lady about to throw. He looked like a guy in a magazine ad, handsome almost. But surely Jo could tell by his eyes. . . .

"Do you really think he's the same man Chark licked?"

"Yes. His eyes are right, and his chin—and he hasn't said a word since he got out on that plank. Not that anyone could have heard him. But if you can get him to talk, I promise you he'll stutter."

Jo hesitated. "I always forget about the stuttering. I guess I didn't notice it as much as you did." All of a sudden, she looked triumphant. "But you're right, he did stutter—and Father Sullivan doesn't. I told you he said mass a couple of weeks ago. Well, he gave the sermon, too. And he did not stutter. Not the least little bit. So there!"

Luke was stopped cold. Logic was on Jo's side but he couldn't forget the wink, that grin. That was Mike up there. Luke knew it. He was pretty sure Mike even knew who he was.

"Don't you see, Luke? You're doing it again," Jo said. "It's like the man in the catamaran you told me about, and the ticket seller just now. You're seeing him everywhere because you want to find him so much. But he's not the right man."

"He is!" Luke said. She had to tell him.

"I'm sorry, Luke. Come on! Let's go see how Bear is. Maybe it's almost time for them to make another announcement?"

"He won't hear it," Luke said. "We can't go off and leave him. No one knows how much more time he's got. We have to tell him now."

"Then *you* tell him!"

Helpless, Luke watched her work her way through the crowd and disappear into the orange tent. For a moment he thought about running after her—maybe trying to convince Mrs. Hill, or track down the Monsignor—but everything he thought of would take time. Paul would believe him but it would take a half-hour to get out to the country club and ten or fifteen minutes for them to drive back.

He glanced at his watch. It was after one o'clock.

"Are you in line to dunk the priest?" asked a woman in a red dress.

Luke shook his head. Once again he pushed through the crowd, then jogged around the outskirts of the festival grounds until he was about level with the ladder propped against the outside of the dunking booth. The area was roped off—no one allowed in but the boys collecting balls—but Luke was ready for that. After he ducked under the rope, he kept right on going across the grass to the tall wooden dunking tank, running low to the ground.

The ladder was only hooked over the tank and it wobbled as he climbed it. Luke's legs wobbled, too, and he could feel one knee beginning to shake the way it had in the police station so that the ladder seemed to beat a tattoo against the side of the tank.

He could hear the loud voices of the crowd—knew that everyone could see him now—that everyone was wondering what he was up to—but he kept his eyes on Mike. The priest still didn't know he was there. Luke hung onto the side of the tank, trying to steady the ladder, wishing he knew what to do next. All he could see was Mike's back, his broad shoulders beneath the wet T-shirt, the short hairs on the back of his neck.

The familiar sense of foreboding—almost of panic—washed over him. Luke cleared his throat, fighting against it. He told himself he could call to Mike. Told himself that he'd talked to more people this past week than he'd ever talked to in his life. But it didn't work. Didn't help. Hanging there on the side of the dunking booth on a rickety ladder in front of a couple of hundred people, he didn't have a prayer. Without turning his head, he could feel all the eyes watching him.

He opened his mouth, but nothing came out.

The live music started up with a blast from the bandstand—one loud chord and a crash of cymbals. Luke licked his dry lips and held tight to the top of the tank, shaking harder than ever. Why hadn't he brought a poster today? Was it because he'd given up? But he shouldn't have given up. Mike was found. Mike was still all right. All Luke had to do was tell him.

He waved one arm in the air, almost falling off the ladder. Mike wasn't expecting to see anyone down here, but he might notice the movement. He had to look down. Luke strained to shout. He knew his face was bright red—knew his mouth was working—opening, closing uselessly. Then he choked out the one word.

"H-hey!"

Mike jerked his head without turning, as if he thought he'd heard something but didn't believe it. Luke could feel the fear closing in on him.

"*Hey?*" he croaked. "Please!"

Mike swung around in surprise. For a second, Luke thought he was going to fall off the plank, but he didn't. The plank swayed back and forth but he was still on it, looking at Luke.

Then he smiled. "Th-Th-Thought I recognized you in line earlier t-t-today," he said, his eyes laughing like he was glad to see Luke again. "How's the p-p-puppy d-d-doing?"

Luke's throat felt like someone had jammed a sock in it. For one nightmarelike moment, he couldn't remember why he was there. The muscles around his mouth began to jump—to twitch, the way his knees did—and he felt as if had fallen forward into the tank and were drowning. He kept his eyes on Mike's face—Mike's eyes—because it was the link between them that kept him above water. With agonizing slowness, he got out the words. . . .

"That—Labrador—The dog that—licked—you. That—dog—had—had—" Luke could have bitten off his tongue in rage. The word he needed so badly to say—the one word that mattered—that would tell Mike what he needed to know—that one stupid, asinine word was the one he was blocked on.

Mike kept on smiling at him. Kept looking at him. Stayed calm. Waited. Interested but not impatient to hear what Luke had to tell him. It was that calm that helped Luke to get out the word.

"Rabies!" he said, in triumph. "Chark had rabies—and he licked your cut hand. So you have to get the shots right away. Dr. Wainwright has the vaccine and we ought to go there right now."

The friendly, accepting look on Mike's face changed momentarily to disbelief; then he seemed to grasp what Luke had told him.

"All right," he said. "G-Give me a few minutes to g-g-get a replacement."

A replacement? Luke almost laughed out loud because it was so funny. But he didn't. Not with everyone staring at them, trying to figure out what was going on. Instead, he backed down the wobbly ladder and stood there, waiting, feeling peaceful.

He'd done it.

CHAPTER TWENTY-FIVE

THE buildings across the water were gold from the afternoon sun, and the bay was a deep, bright blue. The best time of day for Mike to arrive, Luke decided. Feeling completely happy, he picked up the clam rake and waded to shore.

Mike liked raw clams. Luke and Jo had found out a lot about him while they kept him company in Dr. Wainwright's office after he got the shots.

"One injection of immune globulin, one injection of postexposure vaccine, then hang around for a while so I can keep an eye on you," Dr. Wainwright had announced when they walked in the door. Then he added, "And four follow-up shots over a month's time, beginning Tuesday. You tell me what city, what hospital you want to go to, and I'll make sure they have the vaccine."

"How about here?" Father Mike had answered. "Th-That way I can come b-b-back at least four more t-t-times."

It turned out he'd grown up in a little town in the Midwest where all they had was a creek that dried up in the summer. He told Luke and Jo that once he'd set

146

eyes on the ocean, he couldn't get enough of it—and that one hour on their island, with its deserted rocky shoreline and sheltered coves, was better than a month anyplace else. He got excited about the anemones he had seen, and all the pink limpet shells that he'd picked up on the beach at low tide. He said that whenever he saw a big boat go past out in the bay, he waited—counting sometimes—until the waves from its passing beat against the shore. Like a kid. A kid who loved the island. That was when Luke had invited him to stay at the cottage.

"Did you find enough clams?" Jo shouted from the seawall, bringing Luke back to the present.

"Plenty!" He hoisted his bag to show her how heavy it was. There was smoke coming from the barbecue grill, so he knew she had the fire going. Paul was going to do the steaks; Mrs. Hill, the salad and dessert; and the Monsignor was bringing wine. But clams on the half shell were Luke's idea. They'd want the clams first, so he'd better get cracking. Laughing at his own joke, he scrubbed the clams in the sink, then sat down at the kitchen table with a sharp knife and began to pry them open. It wasn't something he was very good at, but he got better as he went on because he had a bunch to work on. Twice—after he figured that Paul had had time to get to the train station on the mainland and back again—he got up to look out the back door, but there was no one coming. When the clams were all open at last, he got the fish platter down from the cupboard, filled it with a layer of the crushed ice that Paul had brought from the club, and wedged the clams, in their bottom shells, into the ice—the way he'd seen it done in restaurants. Right about then he heard Bear bark next door, so he shoved the whole thing into the refrigerator and ran out back.

Bear was right; it was the Volvo. Luke watched Paul get out of the car and lift out a black suitcase—which must mean Father Mike had come. But why didn't he get out?

Uneasy, Luke stopped under the pine tree and waited while Paul came around to open the door on the passenger side. Mike couldn't be sick? The first shots hadn't bothered him. He wouldn't get the next one until tomorrow.

Then a bent-over figure in black slacks and a black shirt backed out of the car. It was Mike, and he was carrying a— a—

Bulldog?

Luke walked closer, staring.

"What d-d-do you th-th-think?" Mike asked, grinning at him. "His name's Judge."

Very carefully, he set his burden down on the grass, and the dog stood there looking around—flat faced and heavy jowled, with a powerful, squat, pure white body and bowed legs.

"He's not very old, b-b-but he's hurt his b-b-back and needs t-to rest up. D-D-Do you th-th-think she'll like him?"

"Who?"

"Mrs. B-B-Bessemer. You t-t-told me how much she missed her d-d-dog, so I th-th-thought—"

Judge lumbered toward him, wrathful-looking but gently appreciative when Luke squatted to rub him behind his wrinkled soft ears. "He seems nice, but what about the birds? Lots of times, they're not in cages."

Paul, who was on the way to the house with the suitcase, turned. "Father Mike tells me the bulldog was raised with pythons and ocelots."

"It's t-t-true." Mike followed Luke and the plodding Judge around to the front porch. "Th-Th-That's why I th-thought he'd d-d-do. His owner had a p-p-pet store in th-the p-p-parish I'm assigned t-to, b-b-but he just d-died. Th-Th-The rest of th-th-the animals were sold."

"But Judge looks like a purebred," Luke said, not understanding.

"He is." Mike grinned. "B-B-But he wasn't for sale. Mr. Roust p-p-put it in his will. Judge worked th-there as sort of a caretaker, you see. I understand he was a p-p-particular friend of b-b-both th-the finches and th-the b-b-big p-p-parrots." Mike's eyes glinted with laughter. "Want t-t-to come with me?"

Luke nodded, smiling. Then he remembered. "The only thing is, she says she doesn't want another dog. Not ever."

"Why d-d-don't we t-t-try?" said Mike with a grin. "We'll be right b-b-back!" he called to Paul, and whistled to the bulldog.

"What do you think Bear will make of him?" Luke asked, smiling as Judge shambled down to the beach, lifting a leg every few yards to leave his scent.

"More t-t-to th-th-the p-p-point, what will th-th-that white rooster make of him?"

Luke threw back his head and laughed, picturing Pee Wee and Judge face-to-face. Yet the bulldog looked as if he could take on anything. "*Were* there big parrots in that pet store?"

"B-B-Big enough. Th-Th-They had b-b-big b-b-beaks anyway." Mike stopped and looked out over the water. "You're lucky, having th-th-the whole b-b-bay in your front yard. Th-Thanks for letting me stay here," he said with satisfaction. "It's worth the b-b-bother of having t-t-to get th-th-the shots."

Embarrassed, Luke ducked his head and led the way across Mrs. Bessemer's long green lawn. He waited until Judge had caught up with them, then he rang the doorbell.

First she peered out, then she opened the screen door and touched Luke lightly on the arm. For Mike she had trouble finding words.

"I'm so—glad—so very glad—that you're all right. Come in!" she urged.

Mike shook his head. "We can't stay now. "Th-Th-The Monsignor's coming t-t-to d-d-dinner. B-B-But I'd like t-t-to come see P-P-Pete t-t-tomorrow?"

"Of course!" She stepped outside and her glance fell on Judge. "Is that yours?" she asked, sounding suspicious.

"No. He's sort of an orphan. I'm keeping him for a while b-b-because his owner just d-d-died."

"Then I'll go ahead and say it," she said determinedly. "That is, beyond doubt, the ugliest dog I have ever laid eyes on!"

"Isn't he?" said Mike, looking smug. "All th-th-the other animals were sold, b-b-but not th-th-this fel-low. It'll b-b-be hard t-t-to find him a home b-b-because he's hurt his b-b-back."

150

Luke tried not to smile. He knew now how Mike was going to do it.

"Hurt his back?" Mrs. Bessemer looked at the dog more closely.

Then, through the screen, Luke saw Hector sidle up to the door and stand there patiently, waiting to be let out. Mrs. Bessemer hesitated, then she opened it for him.

The bulldog and the sea gull seemed to stare at one another, but it was hard to be sure. Both were regal. Hector was immobile. Judge, on the other hand, walked straight inside, sniffed at Hector, and sat down in the middle of the carpet with a wheezing sigh.

"I th-th-think he likes your house," said Mike, struggling to keep a straight face.

"Hey, Luke!" Jo called from the beach. "The Monsignor's here. Mom says for you guys to come now." She waved. "Hi, Mrs. Bessemer!"

Mrs. Bessemer waved back, then she looked at Mike uncertainly.

"His name's Judge. He minds p-p-pretty well. If you open th-th-the d-d-door, I'll call him." He grinned at her. "Or, of course, I *could* p-p-pick him up t-t-tomorrow?"

Mrs. Bessemer gave him a speculative glance, then she looked inside. "You might as well wait until tomorrow," she said coolly. "I wouldn't want to open the door while Sally's sitting on his head."

"DO you think she'll keep him?" Luke asked as they walked down to the beach.

"Only if he's th-th-the right d-d-dog for her." Then Mike smiled a smile that lit up his whole face. "I th-th-think he is, d-d-don't you?"

"Yes!" said Luke happily. Then he saw the Monsignor walking toward them, and, all of a sudden, he felt the familiar tightness in his throat. "I'd better stop off at the house first, I'll see you at the Hills."

"D-D-Ducking out?" asked Mike, raising his eyebrows.

Luke blushed. "I've got to get Paul. And the clams," he added, feeling better as soon as he remembered them. "Clams on the half shell."

"Ummm!" said Mike, licking his lips. "Remember th-th-though!" he warned, his eyes laughing. "P-P-Practice makes p-p-perfect if you want t-t-to t-t-talk t-t-to p-p-people! D-D-Don't d-d-duck out all th-th-the t-t-time!"

Laughing, Luke shook his head and ran up to the cottage.

PAUL was waiting for him at the door. "The folks just called from Athens. They flew there to show some sketches and photos to the experts."

"Is anything wrong?"

"No, but I'm sorry you missed them. They were, too. Dad said they'd call again the first of the week." He hesitated. "I told them what you did, Luke. How you tracked down Father Mike, I mean. They were both pretty proud of you."

Luke's face grew warm with pleasure. He swallowed hard, trying not to let on how good he felt. "How was the wreck?"

"Great! Not too bashed up. And Dad said they've identified the amphorae—the wine jugs—aboard, and it's definitely a fourth-century ship."

"I'll bet he was excited!"

"Flying." Then Paul looked sober. "And Mom said to be sure to tell you again that they *promise* to spend next summer here on the island."

"I know. It's all right now. I'm fine."

"That's what I told them."

For a moment Luke was afraid Paul was going to say too much, but he stopped there.

"What have you done with Father Mike?" he said instead. "And the bulldog? Did Mrs. Bessemer take to it?"

"Father Mike walked on ahead with the Monsignor," Luke said quickly, and went to the kitchen for the clams. "But we figure Mrs. Bessemer will keep Judge." He took the platter out of the refrigerator. "You like him, too, don't you?"

"Judge?"

"Father Mike, stupid!"

Paul nodded, and helped himself to a clam. "Good thing he was dressed like a priest, though. I wouldn't have recognized him from your description." He licked his fingers. "Which reminds me—the Monsignor must have heard him stutter. Why didn't he make the connection?"

"Because Jo forgot to tell him that the man we were looking for stuttered." Jo had always forgotten the stuttering. Right from the start. "Anyway, the Monsignor thought Mike had left the island after they finished picking out the lobster meat for the lobster salad. He didn't know he'd slept on the beach so he could go fishing Sunday."

Luke slid the platter out of his brother's reach and carried it out the door. "What I couldn't figure out was how he managed to give the sermon at five o'clock mass two weeks ago without anyone noticing that he stuttered."

"How did he?" asked Paul, following him.

"He didn't stutter." Luke laughed at the surprised look on Paul's face. "He says he never stutters when he memorizes something or when he's really wrapped up in what he's trying to say. By the way," Luke said as they crossed the lawn, "I changed the sheets on your bed. I figured we'd put him in your room so he could see both the bridge lights and the lights on the other shore. All right?"

"Getting pretty cocky, aren't you?"

Luke could tell Paul didn't really mind. "Well, is it all right?"

"He can have any room you want to put him in, Luke. You found him—and you invited him here."

"Yeah, I did, didn't I?" said Luke, really grinning.

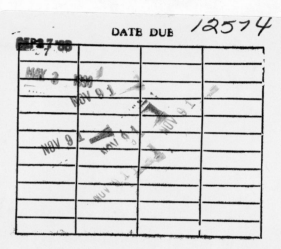
Namovicz, Gene Inyart
To talk in time